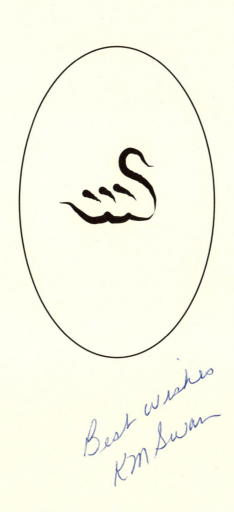

Best wishes
KM Swan

Acknowledgments

To my family, friends and readers of *The Loft* and *Catherine's Choice* who encouraged me to continue writing. To my husband, without whom, *Sarah* would not have been written.

Cover design by

Michael A. Swanson

Sarah

by

K.M. SWAN

Prologue

The yard looked like a Hollywood movie set. Carol turned and went into the house, her two constant companions at her heels. She went into the front hall and sat down on the stairs with one furry friend on either side. Her hands automatically went to stroke their heads. How strange, she thought, we three are the only ones who really know what happened here. They sat quietly together watching the activity through the screened front door.

The coroner was trying to leave, but people kept asking him questions. He had just given a brief statement to the reporter and now was talking to a policeman. The television camera was still rolling and the sheriff was busy giving orders to his deputy. Quite a crowd had gathered by now. It seemed as though every neighbor within six blocks was pushing and straining to see anything they could. Carol was happy to be in the house for the time being. The flashing red lights on the police car cast an eerie illumination in the hallway. She put her head in her hands and tried to block out the clamor when she heard a female voice.

Sarah

"Mrs. Benson?" Carol lifted her head and nodded. A pretty young woman was coming into the house. "I'm Angie Cromwell from Channel Six. We're doing a feature story about what happened here on the five o'clock news tonight. I wondered if you would like to make a statement."

"I really don't know what to say. I'm glad it's over. My family no longer thinks I'm crazy, but it's sad in a way, too. I think I'm going to miss her. Now that really does sound crazy. It's been quite an experience for all of us," she said, as she nodded to the cat and dog beside her. "I think we're all a little tired."

"May I quote you, Mrs. Benson?"

"Carol. Please call me Carol. I'm sorry, I don't think I was very much help."

"Oh, you did just fine. Now be sure to watch the news tonight! You'll be on with your husband and children. It was nice meeting you." She turned to leave, then stopped, looked back and asked, "How did you ever manage to find a cat and dog with matching fur coats?"

Carol thought for a minute and said with a grin. "We had them re-upholstered." Angie turned and went out to the porch laughing.

"See you, Carol!" she called over her shoulder.

K. M. Swan

~1~

They saw the house for the first time while out for a Sunday drive with the kids. Both Doug and Carol spotted it at the same time. It had an "OPEN" sign in the front yard.

"Well, will you look at that!" she said softly, as he slowed down the car.

"It looks like what we've had in mind, doesn't it?" he asked, and stopped the car.

"Why are we stopping here?" Jennifer yelled from the back seat.

"Yeah, this ain't the ice cream store," Troy added to his sister's query.

"Isn't the ice cream store," his mother corrected. "No, it's not, but Daddy and I want to go in and have a look at this house. Would you like to come with us or stay here with Sadie?"

"We'll stay here," Troy grumbled. Just then Sadie jumped up on Troy and gave him a huge wet kiss on his face.

"Stop that, you stupid dog, or we'll leave you out here all by your stupid self." Sadie is part golden retriever and part anyone's guess, with a beautiful

Sarah

golden-tan coat.

"Down, Sadie," Carol scolded. "We won't be long. You three stay in the car now and behave yourselves."

The two grownups got out of the car and went up the walk like kids. They had been dreaming and looking for a place like this for a long time. The house was big, old, and on a large lot. They both loved older houses and often took long drives to look at them. Lately though they were more serious. They really wanted a home of their own, preferably a large house, near a good school where they could settle in and stay. This one looked perfect with its big front porch, long low windows and thick shrubbery.

"Don't get too excited, Carol," Doug told his wife as they approached the porch. "Some of these old dumps should be torn down they're so awful inside."

"Oh, I know that, Honey, but we'll never know if we don't go in."

Carol could hear her mother's voice in her head.

"Why on earth would you waste good time looking at an old barn like that. Do you know what it would cost to heat the place?" May you rest in peace, Mother. We're just looking, she thought to herself as they made their way up the front steps.

"Not bad, so far," Doug murmured. "Looks like the sidewalk has been replaced recently and the porch is in good shape."

"Oh, it looks great, Doug. Look at the beautiful glass in the front door," she said, admiring the thick glass with beveled edges that made up most of the door.

"Take it easy, Honey. We aren't inside yet."

When they entered the house, the realtor called to them from the kitchen. "Good afternoon, folks! Please come in and make yourselves at home. Take a look around and if you have any questions, I'll be right here."

"Thank you. We will," Doug called back.

The front hall was large with a beautiful stairway to the left. A leaded glass window rose high above the hall and cast colored reflections on the rich polished wood of the banister. The living room, on the right, was spacious and had a small fireplace, something Carol had always wanted. On either side of the fireplace were built-in bookcases with glass fronts. Above each bookcase was a window with tiny panes of glass. The dining room had wainscotting below a chair rail. The kitchen was large, too, and had a little pantry with lots of cupboards and a window above the sink that overlooked the backyard.

The realtor merely nodded to them and said nothing, not wanting to intrude. "Is this perfect or what?" she whispered, as they went through the hall and back to the front of the house. "I think it's absolutely charming!"

"Yeah, I like it, too," he said. "Let's go upstairs." The stairway went up to a landing, turned right and continued. There were four good-sized bedrooms that were nicely decorated. There was one full bath in the hall and one half bath off one of the front bedrooms. There were roomy walk-in closets and lots of storage space. A funny little stairway led to the attic.

"What's not to love here, my dear?" she asked,

as she wandered through the rooms.

"I really do like it!" he said, following her. "Let's go down to the basement."

"We should get the kids," she suggested. "I think they'll like it, too."

"I'll go get them," he said, as he started down the stairs.

He went out to the front porch and called to them, but they didn't answer. They were fooling around with the dog, in the back seat, and couldn't hear him. He went down the walk and opened the car door, grabbing the dog's collar at the same time.

"No, not you, Sadie. You have to wait here. You kids want to come in and look at this house? Mom and I really like it!"

"Do you want to, Jen?" Troy asked, not sure if he wanted to or not.

"Oh, I guess we can. You want to?"

"Okay. Let's go," he told her with little enthusiasm.

"Roll down the back windows a bit more, will you, Jen? Sadie needs air," Doug said, as he patted the dog's head. "We'll only be a few minutes, girl."

They walked up to the house with their dad. Troy was holding Doug's hand, and Jenny was skipping ahead of them; her long brown pony tail bouncing against her shoulders. She had her dad's thick brunette hair, while Troy's was more blonde like his mother's, with streaks of red.

"I want you to see inside and tell us what you think. Mom and I think it's pretty nice."

Meanwhile, Carol wandered around the side of

the house to the backyard. A flagstone path led the way. The yard was quite private. It had one huge maple tree almost in the middle of the yard, and the perimeter was lined with hedgerow. There was even a small gazebo in the back corner of the yard. That could use a coat of paint, she thought, as she walked toward it. There were loads of peony bushes in the back and hollyhocks were growing next to the gazebo.

This is the place I've always dreamed of, she mused, silently. She hoped that they could afford it, as she thought she could make a lovely home here. She stepped inside the gazebo and sat on the bench. What a great place this would be to read a good book or just sit and have a cup of coffee. Suddenly she felt dull. She had two kids and stayed home with them, having no outside job, but it was what she had chosen. Her mother would never have understood. No, Mother, you were a doer and a goer, she thought, as a soft breeze caressed her face. I often wonder how you found time to have two kids. Thank heaven for Dad, he made home seem normal. He was always there for Tom and me when you were out doing your thing - whatever it was at the moment. How odd it is when both parents are gone. The two people who were there from day one. She was lost in thought, and shook her head a bit when she heard Doug.

"Carol! Carol, where are you?" he called, coming around the side of the house.

"I'm out in back," she called back. "Come see how nice it is."

"Hey, Mom! We went in the house and it's awesome!" Troy told her.

"Oh, Mom, we really like it. I know what bedroom I want already!" Jennifer said.

"Oh, you do?" Carol said with a smile.

"I think we should check out the basement, don't you?" Doug asked.

"Yes. You kids come, too. Sadie will be all right for a few more minutes," Carol said as they headed back to the house. "Oh, I hope it doesn't have a limestone foundation. I hate that. It's so messy."

There was a door on the side of the house. They opened it and went in. To the left, a few steps went up into the kitchen. To the right, a stairway led to the basement. They went down and found the walls were cement block, not limestone.

"I'm glad for that", Carol said. "And the paint here looks so fresh and clean. Someone really loved this house," she said. "It certainly has been cared for."

"You're right, Carol. And look here, a new electrical box and the furnace can't be more than a few years old. This must be where the old coal bin was. See the marks on the floor where they took down the sides? That window there," he said, pointing, "is where they would put the chute in when they delivered the coal." They walked around the basement, taking it all in.

"I wonder what this patch of cement is on the floor," Doug said. There was a rough patch of cement close to where the laundry hooks-ups were. "I can't think of what it could be," he muttered.

"I don't know," she said. "Maybe it had something to do with a floor drain. All I know is that I love this house!"

The kids were running around the furnace which was in the middle of the basement. "We could ride our bikes down here, Jen!" Troy yelled. "I love this place! We should go look at the attic," he suggested. "Did you see the funny steps going to it? Come on, Jen, let's go look."

"I'll go with them," Carol said. "Why don't you go ask the realtor about the price and we'll go up."

They all climbed the steps; each of them was excited and making plans.

The realtor was sitting at the kitchen table reading the Sunday paper.

"Well, what do you think so far?" he asked. "Oh, and these must be your little ones, right?"

"So far we like the house," Doug told him, trying not to sound too eager. "And yes, these are our kids. Jennifer here is seven and Troy is five," he said, putting his hands on their shoulders. "They think they should go up and have a look at the attic with their mother, if that's all right with you," he said to the realtor.

"Perfectly all right" he said, standing and extending his hand. "My name's Clifford Krause." They shook hands as Carol and Doug introduced themselves. "You two go on and take your mother up. There's a light switch just inside the door on the left. Should be on, but you know how some people are; can't leave a light on if they leave the room. Habit, I suppose. Doug, have a seat here and I'll go over some things with you. We can fill your wife in when she gets back."

Carol excused herself and went upstairs with the

kids.

"Mom I want to show you the room I love!" Jenny cried, as she ran up the stairs two at a time, ahead of them.

"How come I can't pick the room I want like Jenny?" asked Troy, starting to pout.

"Honey, we're just looking," Carol said, taking his hand. "Jenny wants to show us the room she would like if we lived here, that's all."

"It's this one!" Jenny called, as she ran into one of the rooms that faced the front. "It's real big, and look at the cool windows. I could lie on my bed and look out, they're so low. And look Mom, a little bathroom!" she said, nearly shouting with excitement. "Troy look! The closet is so big you can walk in and turn around with your arms out like this," she said, spreading her arms and giving a twirl to demonstrate.

It really is a nice room, Carol thought. It was in the southwest corner of the house. A huge maple tree in the front yard would provide protection from the intense setting sun at the end of the day. A room with a bath would be nice for a little girl, even though it was only half a bathroom.

"Hey, you two, we're suppose to be checking out the attic, remember?"

"Yeah, let's go check out the attic. I know the way!" Troy said. "Follow me," he added, as he hurried out of the bedroom to lead the way.

The stairway was in one of the bedrooms at the back of the house. The door was in a wall of wainscotting and was barely visible when closed. That's clever, Carol thought, as she opened it, and then noticed a matching door at the other end of the wall.

"Jenny, what's in that door?" she asked.

"What door? Oh, I didn't even see it," Jenny said, as she opened it. "It's a closet. Not one you can walk into, though. Just a regular one."

"Well, if that isn't something," Carol murmured, as she started up the stairs. The stairway was very narrow and the steps were small.

"Be careful, kids. There's no railing and these steps are really small," she said, as she guided them ahead of her. There were floor boards down the center of the attic, but on the sides where the roof slanted, there were none, and the insulation was showing. "We have to walk on the floor in the middle here. If we step off, I have a feeling we will go crashing through the ceiling downstairs."

"Oh, that would be cool!" Troy whispered.

"It would not be cool at all. It would be very dangerous!" Jennifer said, in a grown up voice that she used a lot lately. They walked the length of the attic, careful to stay on the boards, and looked out the windows in the peaks of the house.

"This is cool! We're a million feet up, I think!" Troy gasped.

"Well, not quite," Carol said, as they walked back to the stairway and gingerly made their way down the steps. "Let's go find Daddy, it's getting late." They met up with him in the front hall. He and Clifford were coming out of the kitchen. Doug had a big smile on his face and a hand full of papers.

"Carol, I think we'd better go. I'll tell you everything we went over later. I thank you very much,

Clifford," he said, shaking his hand. "We'll be in touch."

"Nice to have met all of you. I have a feeling I'll be seeing you again, soon," Clifford said, as he walked them out to the front porch. "This is a great porch, and see how nicely it's shaded by that old maple tree."

"Yes, it's beautiful," Carol said. "It must be a pleasure to show a house like this."

"Sure is! And say, isn't it a nice day?" They nodded in agreement and made their way down the porch steps. Clifford watched them go and waved. "I'll be talking to you folks. Take care now!" he called.

Sadie had been sleeping, but now was jumping around the back seat as they approached the car.

"Hey, Sadie girl. Wish you could go inside and see the house. I know you will love it. You can lie on my bed with me and look out the window. Ugh, you give such wet kisses!" Jenny cried, wiping off her face.

"See, Mom. Jenny did pick out her own room!" cried Troy. "That's no fair, Dad, tell her." Doug reached over the seat;

"Sit down and buckle up. Sadie, sit. Good girl. Now, what's all this talk about Jenny's room?"

"Let's talk about it later," Carol offered.

"Yeah, we have to get ice cream. You said we could, and you promised," Troy whined.

"It's pretty late for ice cream," Carol said. "I have a better idea. Let's go home now and call for a pizza, then you and Daddy can pick it up. How does that sound? Okay with everybody?"

"Sounds good. I can't wait to tell you about the house, Carol. Oh!" he said, taking a fast left turn, "Hang on back there, you guys. The grade school is this way; I want to see that, too."

"Is that it?" Carol asked, surprised. "How far is that? Only three blocks from the house? How wonderful! Look at the nice play ground, kids. I don't believe this; it's walking distance from the house. Wouldn't that be great," she said, smiling at him and glancing at her watch. "Oh, I didn't realize how long we were in the house. It's almost dinner time. Pizza is a good idea. Sure that's all right with you, Hon?" she said, as she put her hand on his leg. He covered her hand with his and squeezed.

"Yes, fine. I have so much to tell you. Ten minutes and we'll be home, kids," he said, looking at them in the rear view mirror. They were quiet the rest of the way home, thinking about what they had just seen and trying to imagine what it would be like to live in that house.

Sarah

~2~

"You were very good at the open house," Doug said, as he turned down their street. "Mom and I are proud of you."

It's true, thought Carol, they really are well-behaved. She noticed when they were out in public how awful some kids were and it embarrassed her. She felt bad for the kids and the parents. She was so grateful for her family. The kids were good and Doug was a great dad. I'm very lucky, she thought, although she hardly believed in luck. Not luck. Life is what you make it, her dad always said.

They pulled into the driveway just as Sophie came out from under a shrub. She was stretching and yawning as though she had slept the whole time they were gone. Just then the back car door flew open and Sadie was out. She rushed over to the cat and got down on her front legs with her rear-end in the air and barked, trying to scare her. Sophie gave her a bored look and with her tail in the air, turned and sauntered up to the front door.

The pizza was ordered and the men went to pick it up. Jenny talked excitedly as she helped Carol set the table. She couldn't say enough about the bedroom with the little bathroom.

~~~

After the pizza was eaten, the mess cleaned up, the animals fed, the kids bathed and in bed, Doug and Carol were able to sit down and discuss the house.

"Did you see how excited the kids were?" Carol asked, pouring them each a glass of wine. "Jenny was actually red in the face! I think they're as ready for a change as we are."

"Ah, that's better," Doug said, as he sank down on the couch and put his stocking feet up on the coffee table. "Thank you, my dear. This is just what I need, a little vino."

"Here, put the pillow under your feet, it will feel better," she said, as she settled herself next to him. "This is my favorite time of day."

"Mine, too," he said, putting his arm on the back of the couch, around her. "Did you hear Clifford say the house has been empty for three months?"

"No, I didn't hear anything. I was up in the attic with the kids, remember? Did he say why?"

"Well, it seems an older couple lived there and the man died suddenly. It was too big and too much work for the woman alone, so she moved to a high rise. I guess it was pretty sad for her to leave. They lived there for years - had all their kids there, too. They even went to the grade school we drove by, but that was a long time ago. It's been all remodeled, now," he said, getting up to get the papers he had left on the kitchen table.

He sat down next to her once again and showed

Sarah

her the figures he had.

"This is the asking price. It's not bad. It seems a little high for such an old house, but it's the location that's so great. This is the tax bill for last year, but of course that will change. They had a tax break because they were past retirement. All the utility bills are here from the last year, too."

"I wonder why no one has bought it," Carol said, frowning. "There must be something wrong with it, don't you think?"

"Not really," Doug explained. "Clifford said the kids moved their mother out and then did everything that needed to be done to it before they put it on the market. That's why it looked so fresh and clean."

"Nice kids. I hope ours take care of this old mom when the time comes."

"That, my dear, is a long time away," he said. "Would you like another glass of wine? My turn. I'll get it," he said, getting to his feet.

"Thanks. Just half a glass," she said, handing him her empty glass. Just then ten pounds of fur landed in her lap.

"Oh, Sophie, you scared me. Where were you? I didn't even see you," she said, as she rubbed the cat's ears and under her chin, just the way she liked it. "I love you, Sweetheart. You're ready for bed, aren't you?"

Carol had never had a pet in her life until she married. Her mother had forbidden it. "They smell, they have nasty habits, and carry all sorts of diseases!" she announced when Carol and her brother had raised the question of a possible pet. The answer was "no" and that was the end of it. End of discussion. Carol never realized the love that could form between a human and an animal. Well, she knew now and it was wonderful.

Doug had found the tiny yellow ball of fur by the trash cans one night when he was putting out the garbage for morning pickup. He brought it into the house thinking it may be dead. They had warmed her up, fed her drops of canned milk, and fixed her a bed. When they woke up the next morning, they were surprised to find her in bed with them, on Carol's side curled up tight against her. She had found herself a home. Sadie wasn't sure she was going to tolerate a cat, of all things, in her house, but in time they learned to respect and rather like each other, as animals often do.

"We had better get to bed," Carol said, after finishing her wine. "You have to go to work tomorrow, you know."

"But you don't have to get up; why don't you stay in bed until the kids get up."

"I really like to get up with you. I like it when you eat breakfast in the morning and it's nice to look at the paper before they get up. A moment of peace," she said. Often times he would run out without eating anything and it bothered her. She didn't know how he could work all morning with no breakfast.

"Come on, Sophie. Let's hit the sack. If you let Sadie out, I'll pick up here."

"Sure," Doug said and whistled for the dog. She came from Troy's bedroom where she always slept.

"Come on, girl. You have to go out and pee before

we go to bed," he said quietly to her as they headed toward the back door. "Hurry now, girl, it's late. You don't have to sniff every bush tonight." But of course she did.

Carol was wide awake and he was sound asleep. His arm felt like lead across her hip. She moved it carefully so as not to awaken him and tried to relax. She was thinking about the house; it seemed so right. She hoped they would be able to go back there soon and really inspect it. She began to imagine where she would place the furniture and the kind of window coverings that would look nice. It would almost be like going back in time, living in a small village like that. Even though it was fifteen minutes from where they now lived, she was only familiar with Center Street, the main street in Woodland Village. There is an old-fashioned root beer stand there, and the kids like the fact that a girl comes out, takes your order and brings your food to the car. It also had all the necessities such as a grocery store, hair salon/barber shop combined, drug store, gas station, restaurant, a small bar and a five and dime. All the streets except Center are the names of trees. Their house, as she already liked to think of it, was on North Elm.

She was beginning to doze off when she felt the familiar thump on the foot of the bed. She could hear the soft buzz of Sophie's purring. It took the cat a minute to select the right spot, wash a paw or two, and curl up next to Carol's leg. It was important to her that they were touching. Carol adjusted herself to accommodate her friend and whispered softly, "Good night, Sophie."

Alice

Alice Taylor was a deeply religious person; a devout Christian, and a servant of the Lord. She would often describe herself in just those terms. She devoted three days of her week to the church. She was extremely organized and efficient. She scheduled everything from choir practice to weddings. Once she planned the annual parish picnic, single-handedly. She arranged everything - the food, games, prizes, and picture taking. She even thought to provide small moistened towelettes so "Everyone would have clean hands for lunch." She hadn't missed a thing.

She had a husband, Henry, a son, Tom, and a daughter, Carol. Henry was in the insurance business and had an office in the sun porch of their home. He was there for the kids and he was able to plan his appointments around the Christian duties of his wife.

On Sundays they all went to morning services. After that, they would have brunch at a nearby family restaurant, then home to read the paper and take a nap. Later in the afternoon, they were back to church for vesper services and a light supper of sandwiches and dessert.

Her husband didn't share her zeal for religion. Henry believed if you treated other people the way you would like to be treated, things would just sort of work out. But he did go willingly to church on Sundays. It was easier than trying to make a point of his own

Alice loved to bask in the praise and compliments

she received at those Sunday suppers. She was also very proud of the merit pin she was awarded every year for her indispensable work. Carol would smile when people told her how lucky she was to have such a giving mother. She wanted to scream every time someone said that to her, but of course she didn't. Didn't anyone see that Alice had more time for everyone other than her own children?

It didn't seem to bother Tom or Henry, but Carol was deeply affected. She felt an emptiness inside, like a hole somewhere in her, that was not filled until she had her first child. When she had her second child, the hole was not only filled, it was over flowing. Alice was unaware of any of this and Carol adjusted somehow. It was all she had ever known. It was her entire childhood.

Alice was indeed a zealot for the Lord, but this all ended abruptly when she was diagnosed with breast cancer. She was mad as hell at God. How dare He do this to her? She had given her entire adult life to His work, and now He was burdening her with this awful thing. She expressed these sentiments to Carol, ranting and raving about how unfair it was that He had given her this cross to bear! Carol wondered what had happened to "The Lord never gives us more than we can bear," the phrase she had heard her mother tell so many people who were going through difficult times. She felt anger at her own mother's insincerity.

"Mother, that isn't how it works," she said, softly.

Alice was so angry she wanted to slap her daughter across the face. In the end, it was her attitude that killed her. She didn't care and she didn't fight.

She didn't even try to get well. It was as though she were trying to get even with Him. I'll just die, she thought, then see who does Your goddamned work! It was the first time that word had ever formed in her conscious mind.

Carol stood at the open grave between her father and husband, clutching her own small children standing in front of her. Tears were flowing. It wasn't the loss of a mother, she had never really had that, but now there was no chance that someday it would change as she had always hoped. Alice had not found time to learn to know and love her grandchildren either.

Carol vowed then and there to do the opposite of everything her mother had done. Then she would be a good mother.

I thought girls learned from their mothers, she thought, how to become good mothers. Well, maybe I have. I will not do to mine what you did to me.

"Good-bye, Mother," she whispered. "I love you."

Eighteen months later, Henry followed his wife into death. Some said it was a broken heart. Carol said it was the greatest grief she had ever known.

~3~

"Only ten days 'till we close, do da, do da," Carol sang.

"What's that mean anyway?" Jenny asked. "What do you close?" They were beginning to pack things that were seldom used.

"Well, Daddy and I have to meet with the people who are selling the house, they are the Lesters and Clifford, the man who was at the house when you kids were there and some other people to sign papers saying we will buy the house. Then the deal is closed."

"Then it will really be our house? That's all there is to it?"

"Well," Carol continued. "Then we have to make a house payment every month for the next thirty years."

"Thirty years? I'll be a grandma by then!" Jenny cried.

"You will not. You aren't even married. Grandma's hafta be married, right, Mom?"

"I suppose so, Troy," Carol answered, smiling at her son. "It's not as bad as it sounds, Jen, and it's the only way most people can buy a house. We could never save up that much money. And you don't have to live there thirty years; you can move if you want to."

"Oh, that's not so bad," Jenny said, not really understanding completely.

Everything was working out perfectly. They had put in a bid and the Lesters accepted it. The lease on the small place, where they were living now, was up in two weeks and they had given notice. Carol told the landlord that he could show the place if he didn't mind the disorder of moving. He had been good to them and she hoped he would find a new renter soon.

"Well, we sure don't have to do anything to the place," he told them. "You folks took real good care of it, and I appreciate that. I'll have your deposit ready the day you leave."

The kids were excitedly going through their things, trying to decide what to keep and what to part with.

"It's a good time to get rid of toys that you don't want anymore. We can give them to a charity and some kids who don't have any toys will be very happy," Carol told them. "Nothing broken though, we'll put those in the trash," she added.

The girls, as Carol liked to call the animals, were uneasy. Their normally ordered life was in disarray. There were boxes everywhere that needed to be sniffed and inspected. One of which was claimed by Sophie for an afternoon nap.

"Don't worry, you two. Everything will be all right. We aren't leaving you." Sadie was nervous; things just were not the same. "Come here, girl,"

Carol said, sitting on the floor beside the dog. "You're my golden lady Sadie, and I love you," she said stroking her silky coat. "I wish I could explain all this to you, but you trust us, don't you?" Her answer was a big wet kiss. "Come on, kids, let's get back to work! Grab a box and get started. Not that one, Jen, Sophie is sleeping in there." And so the afternoon was spent sorting and boxing toys.

They were able to get into the house a few days before moving day, so Carol and the kids moved as many small things as they could. They were even able to get the sandbox in the trunk, so Troy could play outside if he got bored.

Carol brought all the laundry supplies at this time, too, and arranged them on the shelf on the wall in the basement where the washer and dryer would be. It was then that she felt a draft of some kind. She rubbed her hand across the back of her neck and checked to see if the windows were closed tightly. They were.

When moving day finally arrived, it went well, and it didn't rain. The kids had been more help than hindrance, which surprised their parents. They had shared a room before, so it was special for them to have their own space and some say as to where things should go.

Jennifer got the room she wanted, the one with the little bathroom. She felt very grownup. Troy had his choice of the room next to Jenny's in front, or the one in back of the house with the attic door. He chose the latter, which was next to the large room that would be his parents'. He had fussed about not having a bathroom, but then decided if he chose the back bedroom, he would be next to the main bath that had a tub; Jenny's didn't.

They now had a spare room which was a luxury, but they weren't sure what they would use it for. It was in the front of the house next to Jenny's room. Maybe a sitting room with a small television would be nice. They would have to think about that.

Carol was fixing lunch and wondering where Sophie was. No one had seen the cat. She was hiding somewhere in the house. They had been careful to keep her in her carrier until they were finished moving things and the doors could be closed. Sadie seemed happy just to be where they were. The kids had given her the grand tour from top to bottom.

She was just about to call everyone to eat, when she heard Doug calling to Troy in the back yard. Troy was kneeling at his sandbox building a sand city by the looks of it.

"Hey, Troy!" Doug called to him.

"What?"

"You know we have a dog?"

"Yeah, so?"

"Well, you have to watch where you walk, Buddy. Go tell your mother you stepped in dog poop."

"Hey, Mom! Dad says to tell you I stepped in dog poop!"

"Don't tell her I said. . . ." Doug just shook his head and smiled.

Carol had heard the whole thing; she was in the pantry and the window was open.

"Nice try, Daddy," she said, laughing. "When you've finished cleaning his shoe, lunch is ready."

It had been a hectic weekend. Everyone worked

hard, and the place was beginning to look like home. By Monday they still hadn't seen the cat, but every morning her food was gone and she had used her litter box. Where could she be?

Carol kissed Doug good-bye as he left for work. The kids still had two weeks of summer vacation left.

"Should we take a walk to your new school today?" Carol asked, as the kids finished their breakfast. She had gone herself the week before to register them. "We could take Sadie with us, too. Would you like that, girl?" The big tail thumped the floor as it always did when Carol talked to her.

"I think she said yes, Mom," Troy said, "Where's her leash?"

"I hung it up on the back porch, Honey. Go upstairs and brush your teeth before we go, please."

"Okay," they said together and raced up the staircase.

It was hot and humid on this August morning. Carol was grateful the Lesters had added central air-conditioning when they replaced the furnace. They hadn't thought they needed it, nor did they think they should spend the money, but their sons had insisted, and they had indeed enjoyed it. And so will we, Carol thought, as she cleared away the dishes from breakfast. She heard the kids scrambling down the stairs.

"All clean!" Troy cried, showing his entire set of teeth.

"Very good," she said. "They are sparkling!"

"Let's go," Jenny called to Sadie, and made her sit down. "I have to hook your leash to your collar." Her tail swished the floor. She was excited to be going somewhere, and didn't care where, as long as she was with them. They locked the doors and left by the side door; Carol slipped the key into her pocket and took the leash from Jenny.

"I'll hold it, Jen. You know she gets a little rambunctious when she's out."

"What's rum-bunches?" Troy asked, puzzled.

"Well, it's a bit like how you get, sometimes," she said, smiling and mussing his hair.

It was a beautiful day, even though it was very warm. The sidewalks were shaded by the large old trees along the streets. They were lucky to have found a house here in this wonderful neighborhood.

"Isn't this great, kids? School is so close by, you'll be able to walk every day when the weather is nice. Maybe Sadie and I will walk up and meet you after school once in a while."

"I think it's too far to walk alone. I'm not walking!" Troy announced, loudly.

"I think he's scared, Mom," Jenny whispered.

"I am not scared! I just ah . . . I'm not scared - that's all."

"We can all walk together at first. Then maybe you'll meet a friend or two who live close and you can go with them," Carol offered.

"I hope I meet a nice girl," Jenny said, "someone who lives around here and we could be best friends."

"I hope you do, too, Jen," Carol said, thinking about her own friend in grade school. Peggy had been her best friend in the world. She loved going over to her house after school. Her mom always seemed happy to see them. She wore jeans and baggy shirts and went barefoot. Carol had liked that; her own mother was always dressed as if expecting company. Peggy's mom would get them each a Coke and they would sit on the back porch and talk about all kinds of things. The kinds of things Carol would never discuss at home. She had learned a lot on Peggy's porch.

"Isn't this a nice playground?" she asked when they arrived at the school. "Do you want to swing? I'll push you if you want me to." She dropped the leash and Sadie lay down in the shade. She would stay right there. She had been to obedience school and was well-behaved, but there was a leash law in Woodland, so they used it. The kids chose the swings they wanted and Carol gave them each a push.

"I want to go high as the sky!" Troy called over his shoulder to her. "Higher, Mom!"

She pushed him as high as she dared.

"It's already getting awfully hot," she said, after they had been swinging for a while.

"Should we go home? I have some laundry to do, and I thought maybe we could finish your rooms today."

"I'm thirsty," Troy said. "Let's make some lemonade. Can we?" Then he remembered and added, "Please."

"We sure can. Come on, Sadie," Carol said, retrieving the leash from the ground. "Are you thirsty, too?"

"She sure is! Look at her tongue hanging out," Jenny said.

"That's how she cools herself, Jen. We cool off

through our skin, but animals are covered in fur so they can't," Carol explained.

"Oh, I didn't know that," she said. "Come on, Troy. I'll race you!" They were half a block ahead of Carol and the dog. When they reached home, they turned and came running back.

"Mom!" they both shouted. "Sophie's sitting in the front window!"

"Oh, good!" she said, walking a little faster. "I wonder where she's been hiding."

When they went in the house the cat rubbed against each of them and was purring loudly.

"I think she's telling us that she likes her new home and that everything is okay," Carol told them.

"But, where were you?" asked Troy as he bent down to pet the cat. "We looked everywhere! You sure are a good hider, Sophie."

"I think she explored the whole house at night by herself and slept in a secret place during the day," Carol said, as she started down the basement stairs. "I'm going to start the wash. I'll be up in a minute, and then we'll make lemonade, okay?"

"Okay, Mom," Jenny said, as she hung up Sadie's leash.

Carol began sorting the clothes when she had the feeling someone was watching her. She spun around sharply and then felt foolish.

"We got the lemonade out of the freezer. Should we start making it for you?" Troy called from the top of the stairs.

"No, wait for me please," she answered. There was nothing worse than something sticky spilled on the floor, she thought, as she turned to look behind

Sarah

her one more time before heading to the stairs.

~~~

Carol was in the backyard hanging sheets on the clothesline. One of the first things Doug had done after they moved in was to put up the clothes poles and string the lines for her. She had to have a line for the sheets. Nothing smelled as good as sheets that had dried outside. As she put the clothespin in the last sheet, she heard someone call to her from the yard next door.

"Hello there," the man said.

She picked up the empty clothes basket and walked over to meet the older gentleman at the hedge.

"Hi. I'm Carol, your new neighbor."

"Nice to meet you. My name is Don Hansen."

They talked for several minutes. Carol learned that Don and his wife had lived there a year or so before the Lesters had moved in. His wife was now dead and his divorced daughter lived with him. She had two kids who were in college, so for most of the year it was pretty peaceful.

"They're getting ready to head back to school soon," he said.

Carol thought she detected a little sigh of relief.

"The Lesters were great people," he told her. "We couldn't have had better neighbors. We used to sit on that front porch of yours for hours, just talking and listening to the radio. When the mosquitos would start to bite, we'd go in and play Pitch at the kitchen table. We had some fun times. I still miss them a lot," he said. "Fred died so suddenly it took awhile for it to sink in, I guess."

"Yes, that is hard when it happens so fast," she

said, remembering her own dad.

"Yeah, it sure is. They were awfully good to me when I lost my wife, too. Don't know what I would have done without them," he said, sadly.

"Well, I'm very happy to know you and I hope we will be good neighbors, too. My husband's name is Doug and we have two kids. They're around here somewhere. Oh, there they are. Kids, come over and meet our neighbor, Mr. Hansen. This is Jennifer and Troy."

"Hi, Mr. Hansen," they both said together.

"You can call me Don. None of this mister stuff for friends," he said, smiling. "Then you can call me Jenny!"

"Well, I'm very pleased to meet you, Jenny and you, too, Troy. I think I'd better let your mother get back to work now. We'll be talking, Carol," he said with a wave of his hand.

"Yes, we sure will, Don." She had a good feeling about him.

When Doug got home from work, Jenny was the first to greet him. She ran outside when she saw his car.

"Dad! Hey, Daddy. Guess what?"

"What?"

"We found Sophie!" she shouted.

"You did? Where was she?" he asked, bending to kiss the top of his daughter's head.

"Well, we walked to our school this morning and when we came home she was sitting in the front window. She acted very happy, too. Mom says she likes her new home."

"She's probably right. I swear those animals talk

to your mother. I've got paint for the gazebo in the trunk. Want to help me with it?" He was headed for the back of the car when Sadie almost flew off the back porch. Oh, she loved that man! Her whole body was wagging with her tail. She was so happy to see him, but she knew better than to jump up on him. She sat in front of him and put up her right paw to shake. He squatted down, shook her paw and scratched behind her ears.

You been good today, girl?" She made a whining sound and gave him a kiss. "You always are, right?" he said, standing and petting her head.

Just then Don came out of his garage. Jenny saw him and called to him.

"Hi, Don! This is my dad." The two men walked to the hedge and shook hands over it.

"Well, you're Doug then. Don Hansen here. Very nice to meet you!"

"My pleasure," Doug said, returning his handshake.

"And this is our dog, Sadie," Jenny added.

"Nice to meet you, too, Sadie," he said, and put his hand out to the dog. "I guess I've met all the Bensons then, right?"

"Well, we have a cat, too. She's the same color as Sadie and her name is Sophie, but she hasn't been outside yet," Jenny told him.

"She's still adjusting to the move," Doug told him.

"Oh, sure. That's a cat for you. They take their time about things," he said. "I'll be seeing a lot of you, I imagine. Nice to meet all of you."

"Same here, Don," Doug said, and returned to the car.

Jenny helped take the paint out of the trunk and set it on the porch.

Carol was waiting at the door with a kiss. "What's the paint for, Dear?"

"The gazebo. I think one coat should do it. I don't know when we'll get to it, but when we find time we'll have what we need."

"Good idea. I see you met Don. He seems nice, doesn't he?"

"He sure does, but do you think the kids should call him Don?"

"He told them to. He said, 'no mister stuff between friends.' I thought that was nice," she said.

"Does he have a wife?" he asked.

"No, not any more. She died, but his daughter lives with him. She has two kids."

"How old?"

"College age," she told him.

"No playmates then," he said. "What's for dinner?"

"We're having burgers on the grill and a big salad. It's too hot for much more," she said. "Do you want one or two?"

"Two, I'm starved," he said, pulling off his tie.

"Lemonade or iced tea?" she asked.

"Iced tea, please. I'll go up and change clothes. If you light the grill, I'll cook them for you," he said.

"Ah, you are so sweet," she sighed.

"Ah, I know," he said, laughing. "Where's Troy?"

"In here, Dad," his son called from the living room.

"What are you doing?" he asked, walking over

and dropping down on the couch beside him.

"I'm watching the 'Road Runner.' Do think he'll ever catch him?"

"Well, I watched him when I was a kid, and he hasn't yet. What do you think?"

"Prob'ly not," he said, doubtfully. Doug mussed his son's hair and got up from the couch, looking around the room.

"The house looks nice. Did you kids help your mother today?"

"Sort of. She did most of it herself," Troy told him.

It was starting to shape up. Being much larger than the old place, there were some empty spots, but in time they would be filled. She had put her mother's old drop leaf table in the middle of the dining room. The leaves were up, and it was covered with a pretty cloth. There was a center piece and two candles on it. With the four matching chairs, it looked pretty darn good. In one corner they put the desk, and in another corner there was a built-in china cupboard. Carol had put some beautiful pieces of china and crystal that had belonged to her mother in there. It looked a little bare, but someday they would have a new dining room set. She knew that and she could wait.

~4~

Near the end of the week, Carol met the neighbor on the north side. It was quite early in the morning. Doug had left for work and she was sitting on the back steps with a second cup of coffee watching Sophie. The kids were still sleeping. The cat, outside for the first time, was wary of her surroundings. She was crouching around the hedge, stalking invisible prey.

"Oh, look at the pretty kitty, Cassy!" A young woman was walking to her garage carrying a small child and an enormous diaper bag. She saw Carol and waved. She hesitated a second, checked her watch, and came over to where she was sitting.

"Hi, I'm Debbie Gibbs. So you're our new neighbor!"

"Yes, I'm Carol," she said, extending her hand, then realizing the woman didn't have a spare one to shake.

"Oh, sorry," Debbie said, smiling, unable to shake the extended hand.

"And who is this pretty little girl?" Carol asked.

"This is Cassandra. Cassy for short. She loves

cats. We were watching yours. It is yours, isn't it?"

"Yes, that's Sophie, and she's out exploring for the first time."

"Well, Cassy, we have to get you to day care or Mommy will be late for work. Are you off today, Carol, or do you work the evening shift?" she asked.

"No, actually I work every shift right here. I'm a stay-at-home mom."

"Oh, God, are you lucky. I have to work. Well, it was swell meeting you. Maybe we could get together sometime and visit. I'm not sure when it will be, though. My schedule is so hectic, you wouldn't believe it! Wave bye-bye to the nice lady, Cassy!"

"Bye, Cassy. It was nice meeting you both," Carol said, waving to them. Luck has nothing to do with it, dear Debbie, she thought to herself. It is a choice. She sat for awhile and finished her coffee.

"Mom! Where are you?" It was Troy; he had just gotten out of bed.

"I'm out here, Honey."

"What are you doing ?" he asked, sitting down close to her on the step.

"I'm watching Sophie. She's behind that bush. I think she's chasing a bug." He hugged his small knees and peered to where his mother was pointing.

Jenny appeared in the doorway, rubbing her eyes. "What are you guys doing?" she asked.

"Watching Sophie chase a bug," Troy told her.

"Who let her out?"

"I did, Jen. She was crying at the door. She wanted to go out," Carol told her.

"But what if she runs away?"

"Oh, I think she'll be okay, but maybe we should keep an eye on her today. You kids hungry? You both slept late, didn't you? Pretty soon we'll have to get up early for school," she said, tickling her son. "How about some pancakes?"

"Yeah! I could eat a hundred, I'm so hungry," Troy said.

"Well, I think we'll start with three. How's that?"

They were eating in the kitchen while Carol cleaned up the pantry.

"You know if I went to work like Daddy, we could get new dining room furniture and lots of other stuff," she said, wondering what their reaction would be.

"We have dining room furniture, Mom," Jenny said, with a puzzled look. "What other stuff?" Troy wanted to know.

"Oh, I don't know. Maybe a nicer car," she tempted.

"We have *two* nice cars," Troy said, starting to sound a little worried. "And then who would take care of us?" he cried.

"Oh, I guess you could go to a neighbor's after school until I got home from work. Lots of kids do that," she said.

"Mom, are you just being silly or do you want to work?" Jenny asked very seriously.

"I'm just being silly. I think we're very fortunate that I don't *have* to work, because lots of moms do."

"We shore are!"

"It's *sure*, Troy. A shore is at the lake," corrected his sister.

"Well, that's settled then. What should we do

today? You don't have very many days left before school starts," their mother reminded them.

They decided to go up town to the five and dime store and have lunch at the root beer stand. This would be a fun day for these kids. How would she ever be able to keep these values in them as they grew older in this crazy world, she thought as they all piled into her ten-year-old car. She smiled, thinking of Troy saying, "we have two nice cars." Her Dad had convinced her to buy a new car.

"You don't need to buy someone else's problems. Buy new and you'll get your warranty and all that," he told her. He was right, as usual. She wished she could tell him she was still driving it.

~~~

School started with the usual first week of half days, and of course never the same for both kids. By the second week they had a regular schedule. Jennifer was in second grade and went to school all day. Troy went to kindergarten in the afternoon. At first Carol walked with them or drove them every day, but in one week, Jennifer had a new friend named Allison. The two girls would often walk home with Troy after school. Sometimes Carol would walk with all the kids and the dog to school and then she and Troy would go back home for the morning.

Jennifer could go home for lunch or pack one and eat at school. That was decided the night before on the phone with her new friend. Allison lived on Maple, the next street over. You could go down the alley and be at her house in fifty-two seconds, if you ran, Jenny said. The girls had timed each other. They were nearly inseparable, these two, from the first day they met.

Troy talked about two boys that he liked in his class, but wasn't sure where they lived. He was happy to come home to Carol after school. That wouldn't last long, she knew. Troy, like Jenny, had never been to any kind of pre-school, but he seemed to be adjusting well. Everything was new and exciting to him.

The house was awfully quiet in the afternoons. Sadie had moped around at first, but was used to it now. She followed Carol a little more closely, if that was possible. One afternoon, Carol decided to move the storage boxes from the basement floor onto the shelves that Doug had recently built. There it is again, she thought, and turned to look behind her. Sadie was lying on the floor near her and didn't seem to be aware of anything. Now, every time she was in the basement, she felt . . . no, not felt, *sensed*, something. It was subtle at first, but stronger, now.

"This is nuts," she said aloud, walking around the whole basement looking for something. Nothing. She wondered if anyone else sensed it. Whatever *it* was. She felt as though she wasn't alone, but obviously she was. It was weird, and it almost made her shiver at times. She hoped that it would go away, and soon. But it didn't. After a few days, she noticed a coolness at the back of her neck when she started down the stairs. What was happening to her? She was fascinated and spooked at the same time. She wished she could talk to someone about it, but what on earth would she say? Doug would think she was a fool.

And then, she began to spend more time in the basement. She had never taken so long to do laundry, but she couldn't explain it. She felt, at times, a very real need to go down there. She would sit on an old chair that had been left in the basement and do nothing. When the sun shone through the small window above the washer, she would watch the dust particles floating in the shaft of light. At times that light would hit the irregular cement patch in the floor, and she would find herself staring at that. They had never figured out what that was, but at times she felt drawn to it.

One rainy day, after school, she had the kids down there with her. Troy had an old tricycle that he liked to ride. With no doors anywhere, there was nothing to impede the tricycle traffic. He liked to race around the furnace with Sadie chasing after him.

Carol was folding clothes and Jenny was helping. The sensation wasn't as strong when someone was with her, and she could tell that the kids were not affected. She didn't think Doug sensed anything, either, but wasn't sure. She didn't think he would say anything to her if he did; for the same reason, she didn't want to tell him. *Nonsense,* he would say. Well, she thought it was nonsense, too, but there was something . . . . This went on for weeks, and she tried to behave as normally as she could.

~~~

Doug put a split rail fence at the back of the yard and painted it, and the gazebo, white. It looked stunning and served as a reminder to Sadie not to venture into the alley. Next year they planned to plant flowers in front of the fence. Her heart wasn't really in any of this, though and she felt guilty about it. She was so happy to be in this house and she certainly loved her family, but there was this nagging feeling in the back of her mind and it wouldn't go away. It didn't go unnoticed by her family either. "Dad, what's the matter with Mom?" Jenny asked one day. "She seems different, lately."

"Yeah, she acts really weird sometimes. A-specially in the basement!" Troy added.

"Oh, I think maybe your mom's just tired. Moving is a lot of work, you know," Doug explained.

"She's happy though, right, Dad?"

"Yes, I think she's happy, Jen." He loved the way they were concerned about their mother, and wondered if he believed what he said himself. She certainly had been preoccupied lately.

~5~

"Mom, can Allison stay overnight sometime?" Jenny asked after school one day. It seemed as though the two girls couldn't get enough of each other.

"Well, I guess so, but I'll have to talk to her mother first," Carol replied.

"Her mom's real nice; she works two days a week. Allison has an older sister so she can go home after school and she's not alone."

"Find out what days her mom is home and I'll give her a call." This would be Jenny's first overnight guest and the girls were very excited about it. Allison's mother gave her permission after talking with Carol on the phone. Then the planning began.

"You'd think they were going on a trip," Doug said, after hearing Jenny on the phone with Allison.

"Well, it's exciting, Dear," Carol told him. "It's the first time Jenny's had a friend overnight. We never had room before."

Allison came over after school on Friday, slept over, and stayed all day Saturday. The girls spent a lot of time upstairs. Allison loved the bathroom off Jenny's bedroom. They gave their dolls baths in the little sink.

The spare room upstairs had been made into a den. The furnishings were just odds and ends, but it was a cozy place to watch television. This weekend it belonged to the girls. It became their living room. They had played house all day. Carol didn't think little girls did that anymore, and remembered how she and Peggy had played on her porch with their dolls for hours. She stayed out of the basement all weekend, but Monday there would be more laundry to do.

~~~

Once or twice a week, when the kids were both in school, Don would walk over to Carol's and they would visit over coffee. They both enjoyed the company. He reminded her of her dad. They had gotten to know each other over the weeks and felt comfortable just sitting and talking. He never pried, and he was a good listener. More than once she considered telling him about the feeling she had when she was in her basement, but then didn't. She was sure he would think she was crazy and might not come over anymore. She would miss him, and didn't want to risk it. When she knew him a little better, maybe she would.

This particular day they were on the back porch discussing whether or not it could be screened. It was only big enough for a couple chairs with a table between, but it would be nice if it were bug-free. Don had just explained how it could be done and that it wouldn't be too difficult or expensive, when he turned to her and asked, "Are you feeling okay?"

"Yes, I'm feeling fine. Why do you ask?"

"You seem distracted and sometimes far away. I just wondered if maybe you weren't feeling well."

"Oh, I think it's just moving, school starting and all that kind of stuff," she said, and knew by the look he gave her, he didn't buy that for a minute.

"Well, I'd better get the sheets hung out. Thanks for coming over, Don. It was a nice break."

"Thank you for the coffee. I have to go, too. My daughter asked me to take pork chops out of the freezer for dinner. I'll be talking to you."

"You're welcome. I'll see you soon."

The basement was quiet; the washing machine had stopped. She began taking the wet sheets out of the washer and putting them into the basket when she felt something stronger than ever. A chill went up her spine. What is this, she thought, and how long is it going to go on? She felt like there was something she needed to do, but she didn't know what it was.

Sunlight flooded the room from the window over the laundry machines. She turned to pull the chair over and sit down when she saw something. She shut her eyes and held onto the washer for support.

"Sweet Jesus," she whispered and slowly opened her eyes. There it was. A small ethereal figure; an apparition, she thought it was called. Carol didn't move, nor did she breathe. It appeared to be a small child, but it was hard to tell. It was difficult to make out because it was so sunny. It sure looked like a little kid. Could it be? She rubbed her eyes, unable to comprehend what she was seeing.

It resembled a little girl. Maybe about Jenny's age. Oh, dear God, she thought. What am I going to do? She was almost in tears, but not really afraid. Then it faded and was gone. Carol grabbed the chair and slowly sat down. I don't believe this is happening to me. I don't even believe this kind of thing happens. I must be coming down with something or I'm losing my mind, she thought. No one will believe me. I think I must have imagined the whole thing. I'm just tired, and the way the sun shines so brightly, it *looked* like a figure. She sat there for quite awhile; then she carried the sheets upstairs and out to the backyard. She could not get what she saw, or thought she saw, out of her thoughts.

"Carol! Hey, Carol," Don called from his backyard. "You okay? You look like you've seen a ghost!"

"Oh, Don! You startled me. Ah, I've got a headache, but I'll be all right," she lied.

"Okay. Just checking," he said, and went back to his gardening.

That's the second time I lied to him today, she thought. Oh, what am I going to do? It had to be the way the sun was shining. It must have been reflecting off of something. It *couldn't* be what I thought. It just couldn't be, could it?

"Mom, we're home!" Jenny called from the kitchen.

"Where are you?" Troy yelled.

She had gone back down to the basement to sit and try to figure this thing out. Nothing more had happened. She was pretty sure she had imagined it and felt much better.

"Hey, you two. Come here and give me a hug. How was school?" she said coming up the steps.

Sarah

"I didn't know you were down there. Why didn't you have the light on?" Jenny asked. They came in the side door and didn't see her sitting there.

"Oh, I didn't need light. I was just sitting there. And besides, it's very sunny down there in the afternoon," she told her.

"Why were you just sitting down there?" Jenny wanted to know. "That's really weird, Mom. I want to know what's wrong with you lately."

"Oh, please. I took something down there to put on the shelf, that's all," she said, defensively. She hoped the questions would end.

"Hey, Mom. Look what I made," Troy called to her. "We could make a boat or a train, but I like boats best, so I did this. Do you like it?"

"I sure do," she answered, happy for the distraction. "You did a nice job with the scissors, too." He had filled in the outline of a boat with coloring crayons; then he cut it out and pasted it onto a colored piece of paper.

"How about if we hang it on the fridge so Dad can see it?"

"Good idea, Mom," he said. "Now, look at this." He had also printed the whole alphabet in different colors on a sheet of white paper.

"This is very good, too! Let's hang it by your boat. We're going to need a bigger fridge," she said, laughing.

"I have spelling words to do, and they all have to be in cursive this time," Jenny moaned.

"Well, that won't be hard, Jen. You write very well, and I'll test you on the spelling. Why don't you wait until after dinner though, you've had enough school work for now."

"Okay. Mom, I told Allison I would call her. Can she come over?"

"Sure. I need to go to the store for milk. We could all walk up town, if you'd like. Troy could go with me, and you two girls could shop around by yourselves if you want," Carol suggested.

"Oh, good. I'll call her!"

"Can Sadie come with, Mom?" Troy wondered.

"You know she can't go into the store, Troy."

"Oh, yeah, I forgot," he said. "What's for supper?"

"Chicken," Carol answered.

"She can come, Mom," Jenny said, hanging up the phone. "She'll be here in a minute. What kind of chicken are we having?"

"Well, we can bake it or fry it or cook it on the grill. What do you think?"

Jenny pursed her lips and thought about it. "Um, I think fried, with mashed potatoes. Maybe we could peel them for you; Allison likes to cook."

"Oh, good. I could use the help," Carol said. I feel much better, she thought as they walked to the store, the girls running ahead and she and Troy behind. It was my imagination, for sure.

"We'll let the girls go alone for a while, okay, Troy? You can help me, and then we'll go to the five and dime." He loved that store. He could always find something in his price range.

"Is it too late for ice cream?" Jennifer yelled from Center Street where the girls were waiting for them to cross.

"No, it's only three-thirty. It's okay," Carol said,

catching up with them. "Come on now, all hold hands when we cross. Let's see, is half an hour enough for you girls?" she asked.

"Is it, Allison?" Jenny said, checking with her friend.

"Sure, it's fine," Allison said, nodding her head.

"All right then. We'll all meet here at four o'clock, okay?"

"Right," the girls said together. Troy headed for the door to the grocery store when Carol took his hand.

"We'll get the milk last, Honey. Then it will be cold when we get home. Ice cream or the five and dime first?" He took a minute to think about that. "We can't take food into the dime store, remember?" she said.

"Let's go there first then," he said. "Then we can eat our cones on the way home."

"Good thinking, Buddy," she said. She *had* to have imagined what she saw in the basement.

~~~

Carol was preparing the chicken to fry and the girls were peeling potatoes.

"Allison, you certainly do that well," she said, admiring the precise way in which she handled the vegetable peeler.

"Thanks. My mom taught me," Allison replied.

"Do you like chicken?" Carol asked.

"I love it," she said, grinning.

"Well, do you think you would be able to stay for dinner? It seems to me that you've earned it."

"Oh, thanks, Mom," Jenny said, with a big smile.

"I think we have enough potatoes. I'll cut them

up while you call your mom to see if it's okay with her," Carol suggested. They all loved Allison. She was polite and respectful. She even played well with Troy, and she loved the animals. She didn't have a pet because her dad was allergic to them, she had said. The kids told her they would share theirs with her. She was getting to know them well.

"Mom! She can stay," Jenny called to her mother from the hall. They were both excited and wanted to know if they should set the table.

"Well, yes. That would be nice, thank you."

"Mrs. Benson, Sophie wants to go out. Is it okay if I let her?"

"Sure."

"Allison gets to sit by me, right Mom?" Jenny asked.

"Of course. I think she should," she said, turning and almost tripping over the cat. "Oh, Sophie! I'm sorry. I thought you were out."

"Well, I opened the door and she just sat there so I thought she changed her mind," Allison said.

"Oh, Honey, cats are funny creatures," Carol said, laughing, as she opened the door for the cat. "Sometimes they cry and cry to go out and when you open the door they sit there. They sniff the air and look both ways before they step out. Then they go out slowly so you have to watch out for their tail."

"Yeah, but when Sadie goes out, she just runs out fast," added Jennifer.

"That's right. Cats and dogs are very different, and it's fun to watch them both," said Carol.

"I'm so glad you have pets, Mrs. Benson. I love

them."

Dinner was delicious and they sat and talked awhile after they finished eating. The kids loved listening to Doug's funny stories.

"Goodness! It's a quarter to seven!" Carol exclaimed. "You girls have home work, don't you? I guess we'll have to end this party. Your mom will be expecting you soon, Allison. I'll clear the table."

"I'll tell you what," Doug said. "Let's take Sadie and walk home with Allison while Mom does that, okay?"

"I'll get her leash," Troy offered.

"Ah, she doesn't need a leash, Troy."

"Yes, she does, Dad. Mom said it's the law here."

"Well, all right. If your mother says."

"It's the rule here, Dear," she said, brushing up against him.

"Thank you for inviting me, Mrs. Benson. Dinner was very good," Allison said.

"Well, I'm glad you could stay, and thank you for helping," Carol said. She wondered if she should tell Allison to call her by her first name, as she seemed almost part of the family.

~6~

It was pouring rain the next morning. Allison's mom called to say she could drive the girls to school.

"You'll have to brown bag it today, kiddo," Carol said, looking out the pantry window. "It doesn't look as though it will clear up by noon. If it's raining when you get out this afternoon, I'll pick you up. Find Troy and wait where you always do. Tell Allison's mom, will you? Hurry and finish your breakfast; they'll be here in a few minutes." She finished packing her daughter's lunch, and as an after thought, added another cookie.

Jenny raced upstairs to brush her teeth and get her jacket. Carol was waiting in the front hall with her lunch and her umbrella when she came running down the stairs.

"Don't forget to tell Allison's mom that I'll drive you home if it's still raining this afternoon," she reminded.

"I will. I mean, I'll tell her; I won't forget, Mom," she said, giggling and kissing her mother good-bye. Then she ran down the front steps with her umbrella and her brown bag to the waiting car.

Sarah

Carol stood on the porch and watched her go. She's getting so big, she thought.

"Thank you!" she called, waving to Allison's mom as she drove away.

After lunch, she drove Troy to school. It was still raining. She had the afternoon to herself; well sort of, she did have work to do. She loved the spaciousness of the house, but it was a lot to keep clean. That's why it's nice to be your own boss, she thought. She could take her time. One floor at a time was enough. Today it would be the first floor. She was finishing up and went down to the basement to hang the rags on the sink. Sadie was right behind her. Sophie preferred to sit on the landing. There were no backs on the stairs, so the cat would sit there and watch between the steps. Carol thought she did that so she could beat Sadie to the kitchen when they went back up stairs. They did behave a lot like kids, at times.

She hung the rags on the laundry tub and began to wash her hands when she heard Sadie growl. It was a soft low growl in her throat. Carol felt a chill go up her spine as she turned to look at her. The dog was staring straight ahead. Carol turned and saw it.

"Oh, God. Not you again," she whispered. The fur was up between the dog's shoulder blades. She glanced up at the cat on the landing. Sophie's eyes were dilated and she was staring, too. Her ears were flattened against her head. She sees it, too. The basement wasn't bright today and Carol could see much more clearly than the last time she saw this, but oddly, she wasn't afraid. She knew it wasn't her imagination now. She also knew, for sure, that the animals saw it, too, or at least sensed something.

It was definitely a little girl. She had long hair and was wearing a long dress, or maybe it was a nightgown. Her arms were straight down at her sides. Carol smiled, she felt no threat. Sadie was still watching and so was Sophie, but they no longer looked as though they felt threatened either. Carol felt warm and full of love . . . yes, that's what she felt. It was love.

How could this be happening? She didn't even believe in this paranormal or parapsychology or whatever the hell it was called. But now she knew it was not imagined. She had witnesses, too. Oh, great. *Mute* witnesses. It didn't last very long and then the girl simply faded away. She had been standing on the patch of cement in the floor.

Thank God the rain had stopped. She didn't have to pick up the kids, but still she didn't have much time. She ran up the stairs, grabbed a pitcher of iced tea from the fridge, two glasses from the cupboard, and took them out to the gazebo. Don was working in his yard as she knew he would be.

"Don," she called. "Want to take a break and have a cool drink with me?" It was September and still very warm outside.

"Don't mind if I do. Thanks," he answered, leaving his work and walking to her yard. He sat down inside the gazebo and wiped his forehead with a handkerchief.

"Sure is a warm one today. That rain made it feel like a steam bath," he said, taking a long swig of tea. "This is so nice with the new paint; the fence looks great, too. Don't know if I told you or not." He looked at her closely then. "Carol, are you okay? You just don't look right," he said, putting his hand affectionately on her arm. He really liked this girl. He had from the start. "Can you tell me about it?" he asked. Her hand shook as she poured tea into her glass.

"Don, you have to help me," she said, her voice shaking. "What do you know about the people who lived here before the Lesters?"

"Why? What are you talking about?" he said, taking a sip of the tea.

She told him the whole story.

"Oh, Honey, you must have imagined that," he said, staring at her in disbelief. She looked darn serious, though, he thought. "What does Doug say?"

"I haven't told him yet," she confessed.

"No one sees this but you?" he asked.

"Well, that's just it. Today Sadie and Sophie saw it, too. I know they did. That's how I know it's real and not my imagination," she told him.

He shook his head in disbelief. "Carol," he said, taking her hand, "I think you should talk this over with your husband, not me."

"Don't look at me like that, Don," she quipped. "You know me well enough to know that I'm a pretty stable person, and I'm not an alarmist. And to tell you the truth, I have never believed in this kind of thing myself, but I'm telling you what I saw. So don't patronize me!"

"I didn't mean to do that, Carol," he said, sincerely. "But what would those people have to do with what you just told me?'"

"I don't know," she said, frustrated. "I just have to start somewhere."

"I think so much of you and your family; I'll help if I can. Now give me a minute. I think the name was . . . . Oh, it's been such a long time," he said, looking upward and rubbing his chin. "Lorence! That's it. Inez Lorence was her name, and he was, ah, what the heck was his name. He was a mean son of a bitch, I can tell you that. I beg your pardon for that, but he was." He thought a minute more. "Clyde, that's it! How could I ever forget? He was mean as the devil. That woman had more bruises than a prize fighter. My Mrs. said we should mind our own business; that's what you did in those days."

"Did they have any kids? Can you remember?" she asked.

"Well, now that you mention it, there was a little girl there for awhile. 'Bout the age of your Jenny, I think," he said, staring at her.

"What do you mean, for awhile?" she wondered.

"Well, that's what was strange. We saw her now and then, but she was real shy, and would barely speak. Our kids thought there was something wrong with her. She must have stayed inside a lot, because we didn't see much of her. We thought that maybe she was a visiting relative at first, but then our kids would see her walking to school, so we knew she lived there. She always walked alone, and she wasn't in any of our kids' classes, so they didn't really know her at all. Clyde would barely speak when we saw him, and Inez acted like she didn't dare speak to us," he told her.

"But what did you mean, the girl was there for a while?" she asked again.

"Oh, right. Well, after a while we didn't see her at all. Our kids never saw her walking to school, either. Shortly after that, they up and moved. Then the Lesters moved in and we just sort of forgot about them, I guess. We were so happy to have nice neighbors. I wonder whatever happened to that quiet little girl. Sarah. Her name was Sarah. I just now remembered that," he said.

"Were you ever down the basement, Don?"

"Oh, I suppose so . . . . Yes, I helped Fred Lester take down the sides of the coal bin. Gee, I'd forgotten all about that."

"You wouldn't remember seeing a cement patch on the floor would you? It's near the laundry tubs."

"Seems to me that they had an old rug by those tubs. They had a dog that liked to lie there and sleep in the sun."

"Well, there's a patch of cement there. I just wondered if you knew what it is. That's where I see her," she said, quietly.

They sat without talking for a few minutes, lost in their own thoughts - he wondering what had happened to his neighbor, she wishing that she hadn't told him.

"Mom! Where are you?"

"Out here, kids," she shouted. "Thanks for listening, Don. I hope you don't think I'm crazy. Please don't think that, because I'll probably need to talk to you again. Maybe you can come over and we'll go down there together."

"Sure, Carol, but I think you should tell Doug. Don't think you and I should have secrets from him."

"I understand, and you're right. I'll see you soon," she said, touching his shoulder.

"Hey, you two. How are you?" he called to the kids.

"Hi, Don. We're good," they said.

"Mom, you know what?"

"What, Troy?"

"There's this kid in my class named Jason and you know what?"

"No, I don't, Troy. What?" she asked, smiling at him.

"He lives down our street!" he exclaimed.

"How do you know?" his mother wondered.

"We saw him when we were walking home from school today. His mom picked him up at school and we saw them stop at that green house down the block. You know that green house, Mom?"

"I think so," she said, trying to picture the house in her mind.

"Well, that's where he lives. Do you think he could come over sometime?"

"Well, I don't know why not. Maybe if you get to know him, his mom will let him walk home from school with you. If she knows you have an older sister, she just might," she told him.

"I really like Jason. He sits by me in school and sometimes we're partners when we do stuff," he said, excitedly.

"Then I think we should get to know him well," his mother said.

Sarah

~~~

Many days had passed and Carol saw the girl often. She began to talk to her.

"I wish you would appear to just one other person. It would help so much if you could. No one will believe that you're real, you know. I *know* you need something, but I don't know what it is," she whispered, softly to the nebulous form. Whatever the animals perceived this to be, they were comfortable with it. Carol watched them closely when they were with her. They stared where she appeared every time.

"I wish you could help me out here a little. Sometimes I do wish you could speak," she said, as she stroked the dog. Sadie gave a little yelp at the word speak. "Yes, you do speak very well, girl. What do think this little girl needs, Sadie?" A kiss was her answer. Slowly the form began to fade. "Sarah? Is your name Sarah?" She was gone. Carol climbed the stairs - this was really beginning to get to her. She still hadn't told Doug. I have no idea what to do with this, she thought, as she went out to the back porch for some fresh air. Sophie was draped over the porch rail, dozing in a sunny spot.

"Do you ever worry about anything, Soph'?" Carol asked. The cat opened one eye and sighed. "Oh, I suppose that would be beneath you. Cats can be such snobs," she mumbled and sat down on the top step, staring at nothing for a minute or two. Debbie pulled her car into the garage, and soon she came out around the back, laden with the kid, diaper bag, huge purse and what looked like a small suitcase. Carol had never seen the woman without her arms full. When Debbie saw her, she dropped everything but the kid and walked over.

"Hi, Carol. Watcha' doing?"

"Not much; just waiting for the kids. They should be home from school soon."

"God, I envy you so much. Isn't it nice to just stay home all the time? I mean what do you *do* all day?" Cassy began to squirm in her mother's arms. Carol put her hands out and the baby went right to her. She was a beautiful child. I don't think I could leave you all day if you were mine, you sweet thing, she thought, nuzzling Cassy's head.

"I'm home early today because I had a dentist appointment," Debbie told her. "By the time I got out of there, it wouldn't have paid to go all the way back to work, so I just picked her up and came home. I know they'll dock my pay, though, and that sucks!"

"Well, it won't be much, will it?" Carol asked, she was only an hour early getting home.

"Every little bit counts you know! Well, I guess you don't know, since you don't have to work."

Don't go there, Carol thought, as she smiled at her neighbor. I'm in no mood for your whining today.

"Well, Sweetie, we'd better go. You can play in your playpen so I can get something done. Tell Carol bye-bye."

Carol was tempted to ask her if the baby could stay, but didn't. Maybe another time when she was in a better mood. Now she's going to put her in the playpen to play alone. "I just don't get it," she murmured, remembering her own childhood. But I'm the lucky one. Ha! If I drove a car like yours, lady,

I'd have to have two jobs to pay for it. "Shit!" she said, walking into the kitchen.

"Hey, Jenny. Mom said SHIT!"

"So did you!" Carol said, spinning around to face her son. They had come in the front door and she hadn't heard them.

"I'm telling Dad!" Troy announced.

"Oh, Troy, Mom's just upset. You're upset a lot lately, Mom. How come?"

"I'll be all right, Honey, I promise. How was school today?" She couldn't go on like this much longer. She would have to tell him tonight.

~7~

They were sitting on the back porch sipping decaffeinated iced tea. The kids were bathed and in bed. They decided that they would screen the porch next spring. It was small, measuring only twelve by seven feet, but it was perfect for two people to sit and enjoy the outdoors without the annoyance of bugs.

"You know, a day bed would fit perfectly at the end of the porch there," Doug said, gesturing with his thumb. "They're usually about six feet long, I think. What a great place that would be to take a nap!" He turned to look at his wife; she was in another world, it seemed. "Did you hear me, Carol?"

"I'm sorry. What did you say?" she asked, trying to appear interested.

"I said, a day bed would fit on the end there," he repeated.

"Oh, yes it would. It would be a nice place to nap. I know Sophie would love it," she said. She hadn't heard a thing.

"We could hang a bamboo shade there, too," she added. "It would make it nice and private." She took a drink of her tea and stared straight ahead.

He wondered what was bothering her. He slid his chair closer to hers and put his arm around her shoulders.

"Are you okay? You seem like you're somewhere else," he asked, quietly.

"I'm all right," she said, but he wasn't convinced.

"Do you want to talk about it?" he asked. "It might make you feel better," he suggested.

"I doubt that!" she said, emphatically. He took his arm from around her and turned to look at her.

"And why is that?" he asked, trying to be patient with her.

"Because you'll think I've lost my mind - that's why," she told him.

"What is it, Honey? You can tell me anything, can't you?"

"This is different," she said. Her throat began to tighten and she hoped that she wouldn't cry.

"What could be so bad? Aren't you happy? You like the house, don't you?" he asked, totally confused.

"I love this house; you know that. Remember you said that I acted differently lately?" she asked, now facing him and looking him straight in the eye.

"Well, you have been acting differently sometimes. I didn't say it was bad, just different," he said, not wanting to anger her, now.

"Do you really want to know why?" she asked.

"Yes, I really do," he said, hoping to get on with it.

"Please don't make fun of me," she said, seriously.

"I promise," he said, grinning and holding up his

right hand. Then he stopped. He could see how serious she was.

"I've been seeing something in the basement," she said, softly.

"*Seeing something?*" he repeated, now puzzled even more.

"Yes! It's a little girl."

"There's a little girl in our basement," he stated.

"Yes," she breathed.

"And you haven't said anything to anyone?"

"I couldn't," she answered, staring into the yard.

"Who the hell is she?"

Her answer was a shrug of her shoulders.

"Did it occur to you that her parents may be looking for her?" he asked, raising his voice.

"Shh," she whispered. "I don't want the whole neighborhood to hear! It's an image or a phantom or something . . . I don't know," she said, sounding defeated.

"You mean a ghost, right?" he asked, with a tone that she didn't like at all.

"Yes, I suppose that's what she is."

"You're kidding," he said, staring at her.

"This is exactly why I didn't want to tell you. I know you think I'm crazy. Don looked at me the same way when I told him. Are all men alike?"

"Wait a damn minute! You told this cockamamie story to the neighbor? You just said that you hadn't told anyone. Now you say you told the neighbor? Jesus, Carol," he ranted. "I get the house you want, I put up with your moods for six weeks, and you talk to him and not me. What is that crap, huh? I need a drink." He stamped off into the kitchen.

I knew it, she thought. I shouldn't have said a word. But, how could she not tell him? She didn't know what to do.

He came back with a glass of wine for her and a brandy for himself.

Oh, no, she thought. He didn't drink brandy very often; usually when something had gone wrong or he was mad.

He opened his mouth to tell her just what he thought, but then stopped. She was crying. This woman of his rarely cried. He could count on one hand the times he had seen her cry. Oh, she cried at sad movies, and when her parents had died, of course, but he didn't mean that kind of crying. She didn't cry for no reason, or just to make a point. This must be serious. He put down his drink and stood up. Pulling her to him, he held her very tight.

"I'm sorry," he whispered into her hair. "Don't cry."

"You have to help me," she said, between sobs. "It's the truth. I'm telling you I saw her!"

"How can I help you? I don't believe in that stuff," he said.

"*Neither do I*," she cried. "You have to be patient with me because I have to figure it out. I told Don because I thought he maybe would understand, being older and all, but I don't think he does. He told me that I should tell you. He also told me about the family who lived here before the Lesters." She was still crying and he was still holding her.

"Can you stop crying now?" he asked. "We can sit down and try to figure this thing out. Oh, and by the way, I heard something about you today."

"What?" she asked, looking up at him and wiping her nose.

"Troy told me that you said shit," he said, smiling. She was shaking, but not from crying. Now she was laughing.

"That little snot," she said. "He told me he would tell you."

They stayed up awhile longer and talked about the Lorence family. Doug suggested that she go to the public library in town and look them up in an old city directory. Maybe she could find a census taken back then, or something else that would help. The village had a small library, housed in an old store front, but he was sure it didn't have records of any kind.

"That's what I mean by help," she said. "I'll do that soon. Why do you think the animals see her?" she asked. "And why does she always stand right over the cement patch?"

"How can you be sure Sophie and Sadie see her?" he asked.

"I know that they do. The first time they saw her, the fur was up on Sadie's back, and Sophie's eyes were huge and her ears were back. Now, they both seem to be okay with it; they just watch her. I'm not frightened at all either. Actually, all three of us are very comfortable with her being there. It's strange . . . ."

I'll say it's strange, he thought, silently. Like a crazy club of "all three of us."

"The patch in the floor probably has nothing to do with it," he said, not sure where she was going with that.

Sarah

"I'm not so sure about that," she said.

How the hell did she expect him to answer her questions when he didn't understand any of it. When they went to bed that night, he was very gentle with her.

"I love you so!" she whispered to him afterward. "Thank you for understanding."

"I love you, too. Good night," he said. Well, she had that all wrong. He didn't understand a thing about what she had told him.

~8~

The public library in town was about twenty minutes from home. She would leave as soon as Troy left for school. She picked up the phone and called her friend next door.

"Don, this is Carol."

"Well, good morning," he said, sounding pleased to hear from her.

"Can you do me a favor?" she asked.

"Absolutely. What do you need?"

"Will you be home later this afternoon?"

"As far as I know; what can I help you with?"

"Well, I'm going to the library when Troy leaves for school, and I'll probably be back by three. But just in case I'm not, you'll be there, right?"

"I'll be here. Say you're not going to try to look up the Lorences, are you?" he asked.

"Yes, I am. Why?"

"Oh, why don't you just put that out of your mind. You'll get over this thing in time," he said.

"I don't think it's going to go away. I'll let you know if I find anything. Thanks, Don. Good-bye."

Oh, sure, this *thing* will just go away if I put it out

Sarah

of my mind, she thought, as she hung up the phone. He thinks it's all in my head. I think that would be easier, actually.

It was a beautiful fall day and a pleasant ride. She was humming as she pulled up to the stop sign and waited for her turn to go. She thought that she would stop and see Mrs. Lester, if she had time and made a mental note to call first. She drove for twenty minutes listening to the radio. It felt good to be doing something, finally, about what was happening to her in the basement. She hoped that she would get some answers today. Driving into the library parking lot, she noticed a car backing out; she waited and drove into the vacated space. She locked the car and walked to the white stucco building, admiring the huge pillars as she opened the heavy glass door.

The library wasn't busy and the woman at the desk was very helpful. Carol found just what she was looking for - the census for the year before the Lesters bought the house. There was a Lorence family. Clyde, Inez, and a daughter, Sarah. The city directory listed them at 409 North Elm Street. She checked the obituaries for that year and the year after, but found no death. What happened to the daughter? She looked through local history around the same time too, just in case there was a child missing or some such news, but she found nothing. She didn't think she would, because Don surely would have remembered that.

Well, she had found the information that she needed; the girl was indeed their daughter. Don said he thought she may have been a niece or some other relative who was just staying with them when he didn't see her anymore. No one would have dared to ask.

Glancing at her watch, she realized that she would have time to visit Mrs. Lester. She found a pay phone in the hall of the library and looked up the number. She put in the coins needed and dialed. It was answered on the first ring. She introduced herself to the woman on the phone and asked if now would be a convenient time for a short visit.

"Why, yes. I'd be happy to see you. Carol, is it? I'll make a pot of tea. I'm on the seventh floor, apartment 714. Call from the lobby and I'll buzz you through. Oh, this is so nice. I'll see you soon!"

Carol had never met the woman. Mrs. Lester's son, Charles, had taken care of all the real estate transactions for her. I bet she wonders why I'm calling, Carol thought. Well, she certainly sounded happy to be having company. She found the highrise easily and parked her car close to the door. The building was beautiful and the lobby luxurious. She checked with the man on duty at the front desk and was soon buzzed through.

"You wouldn't be Mrs. Lester's family now, would you?" he asked, as the heavy door that led to the elevators opened silently.

"No, I'm just a friend," she said, hesitating a bit describing herself as her friend, but thought it was the easiest response.

"Well, she'll be right happy to see you. She's waiting for you. Have a nice visit."

"Thank you," she said.

She rode the elevator up to the seventh floor and

stepped out to see a woman standing in her open doorway.

"Are you Carol Benson?" the woman asked.

"Yes. And you must be Mrs. Lester," she replied, as she walked toward her, extending her hand.

"Yes, but please call me Edith," she said, shaking Carol's hand, warmly. "Come in and sit down! Tea's almost ready." Edith loved having company and always put out her best teacups and linen napkins when someone came to visit.

"I'm very happy to meet you, Edith, and I want you to know how much we love your house."

"Oh, I'm so happy to hear that. We loved it, too. I was hoping someone would buy it and take care of it the way we did. Fred did a lot of work there, inside and out," the old woman said.

"Yes, we can tell," Carol told her. "That was one of the reasons we wanted to buy it so badly. It's in perfect condition."

"So what brings you back to town?" Edith asked, pouring the tea.

"Well, I had an errand here so I thought I would look you up," she explained.

"Oh, I'm so glad you did. Say, how is Don doing? He hasn't been to see me for awhile. He pops in every now and then. He's a good friend and so was his wife."

"He talks about you a lot, and tells me how much fun the four of you had," Carol said.

"That we did," Edith replied, remembering those happy years. "They were wonderful neighbors. Lemon and sugar?"

"Yes, please," Carol answered. "Edith, Don told

me that he lived there before you moved in, right?" she asked.

"Well, yes, but only for a year or so, I think. That was a long time ago," she said, passing a plate of cookies to her guest.

"It sure was," Carol said, taking a cookie. "These look yummy. Did you make them?"

"Oh, yes. They're my favorites. My own mother made them for me when I was a little girl. I've always had the recipe - don't even need it anymore. I know it by heart," she said, smiling.

Carol took a bite out of the cookie and complimented her hostess. It absolutely melted in her mouth. "Did you know the Lorences at all?" she inquired.

"Who?" Edith asked, puzzled.

"The Lorences. The people who sold you the house."

"Oh, no. The house was in the hands of the realtor; the family had already moved. We did contact them later, but the man had died. We found some old papers on the top shelf of a closet that we thought might be important to them. I don't even know how Fred got hold of the address, as it was out of state. It was six months or so after we had moved in. He talked to . . . oh, what was her name? I can't think of it now," she said.

"Inez?" Carol offered.

"Yes, Inez. That's it. She told Fred that Clyde, now I could never forget his name, had died of cirrhosis of the liver shortly after they moved. Fred mailed her the papers and that's the first and last contact we had with them. Don told us about Clyde.

Sarah

I guess he was a real . . . well, I shouldn't say what he called him. That's why I remember his name so well. He wasn't very nice. I bet I have that address to this day. I've had this book since we married, can you tell?" she asked, laughing, as she reached into a drawer and took out a very worn old address book.

Could I be this lucky? Carol wondered.

"J, K, L, Lorence! I can't believe I saved it!" She wrote the address on a piece of paper and gave it to Carol. "I don't know if you want it or not, but there it is," she said.

"Well, actually I'd like to know something about the history of the house, so yes, I'd like to have it. Thank you," she said, taking the scrap of paper from the woman and putting it into her purse. "Oh, I wanted to ask if you remember a patch on the floor in the basement. It's a cement patch, about this big," she said, holding her arms up to show the size. "Did Fred do that? Do you remember it at all."

"Patch in the floor . . . where in the basement, Honey?" Edith asked, furrowing her brow.

"It's near the stationary tubs," Carol said.

"Oh, that. Yes, it was there when we moved in. It didn't look very old, and Fred thought it may have had something to do with the floor drain. We put an old rug over it and Sandy, he was our dog, loved to sleep there in the sun. He was a cocker spaniel and pretty old by the time we moved in. He had some arthritis, I think. He's buried right out in back by the hollyhocks. Oh, he was such a good dog," she said, smiling and remembering her pet so well. They talked about the house and the neighborhood and how it had changed since Edith and Fred moved there. Their time together had flown by and Carol realized that it was time for her to go.

"Well, Edith, it was a pleasure meeting you. I must be leaving soon because my kids will be home from school. Maybe I'll bring them to visit you some time. They love the house, too."

"Oh, I would like that! They could tell me which rooms they sleep in and how they look now; that would be such fun. Did you say a boy and a girl?" Edith asked.

"Yes. Jennifer is seven and Troy is five."

"Well, do that sometime; it would be nice to meet your children. Please tell Don I said hello, and to stop by if he has time someday. You too, but call first, this old lady still gets out now and then!"

"I'll do that, Edith, and thank you for the tea. Everything was lovely."

~9~

Carol arrived home about the same time as the kids. Troy had Jason in tow.

"Mom, I know I should ask before I invite someone over. If he can't stay, he'll go home," Troy said.

"Oh, it's okay this time. Does his mother know he's here?"

"Yeah, she said he could stay until four forty-five, if it's okay with you."

"Well, it's nice to see you again, Jason," Carol said, smiling at her son's new friend. "Yes, it's fine with me. You kids go and play. I'll tell you when it's time to go home."

"Thank you, Mrs. Benson," Jason said, politely.

"If you want a snack, help yourselves, kids."

"Are you hungry, Jason? I'm starved!" Troy said. Jason nodded, yes, he was, too.

~~~

Carol called information in the town where Inez had last lived. There was no listing for Inez Lorence.

"Perhaps the number is unlisted, Ma'am," the operator offered.

"Yes, perhaps. Thank you," Carol said. Then she

wrote a letter to Inez at the address Mrs. Lester had given her. She included a self-addressed stamped envelope, hoping to ensure an answer. The letter came back in a week. The woman explained that Inez had died three years before and no, she had no children. She was sure of that. She had included her phone number, and asked if Carol was a relative. Carol called her and told her that she was not a relative, but asked if Inez had left any personal belongings. She hoped to find some pictures or records of the little girl, but the woman said there was nothing, just some old clothes. Carol suggested giving her things to the Goodwill charity. They exchanged a few pleasantries, thanked each other and hung up. Carol was disappointed.

~~~

INEZ

Inez grew up in an orphanage. When she was eighteen years old, she was told that she had to leave. She left with a little money, a high school diploma and a suitcase with everything she owned in it. She found a job waiting tables and a furnished room nearby. It wasn't much of an existence for a young woman. No wonder she was so taken when she caught the eye of a strong handsome fellow who often ate where she worked. She waited on him every time he came in and learned to know just how he liked things. She made sure she did everything right. She was thrilled when he asked her for date, and more so when he asked her to marry him three weeks later. It was the biggest mistake of her life.

Clyde Lorence didn't want a wife and partner, he

wanted a slave. He hit her a lot, too. She thought it was because she wasn't doing everything the way he liked. Then when she learned to do everything perfectly, and he still hit her, she knew he *liked* hitting her. It made him feel like a man. When her baby girl was born, she was ecstatic with joy. She had someone to love who would love her back. They were as close as two people could be, but Clyde was indifferent. He neither liked nor disliked the little girl, but he still liked to hit her mother around.

One night, it happened as it always did. He came home drunk and started in on Inez. The girl was awakened and went downstairs. She saw what was happening and cried, begging him to stop hitting her mother. Clyde looked up and saw Sarah standing there, pleading with him. He pushed Inez aside and picked up his daughter. The cellar door was open part way. He kicked it open wider with his foot and threw her down the stairs. She hit the landing and kept going. She landed on the concrete floor and didn't move again. Ever.

Clyde told Inez that if she spoke of this to anyone, the same thing would happen to her. And she was to stay out of the basement until he told her otherwise. Whatever he was doing down there made a terrible racket, but Inez said nothing. Then he stormed up the basement stairs, glared at Inez who was cowering in the kitchen, and went upstairs to Sarah's bedroom where he removed all evidence of the child. He took everything out to the burning barrel near the alley and set it on fire. It was as though she never existed.

After his death, Inez thanked the Lord again and

again for taking him away from her. She went back to her old life, waiting on tables. Every night, since that tragic night, she dreamed of her precious daughter as she slept. Many years later she died in her sleep, as memories of her daughter filled her dreams.

~~~

She was appearing every day now, that is if Doug or the kids weren't down there. Sadie was usually by Carol's side when she was in the basement, but this didn't stop the girl from appearing. Carol was positive that Sadie could see her, too. She could tell, just by the way she would lift her head to look towards the girl when she appeared, and then how she would put her head down on her paw again and doze off. She never seemed alarmed, nor did she show fear; she just took it in stride.

The cat was not very interested anymore, but Carol thought Sophie still saw the girl, as she sat on the landing poking her head between the steps, watching them closely.

"I know your name is Sarah, and now I think I know what you want," Carol whispered, as she sat on the chair watching her. "I'll try to do what you want me to do." She wished she could hold this little girl and tell her everything would be okay. She was pretty sure this kid had come to a violent end.

After dinner that night, Carol told Doug everything that she had discovered about the Lorences.

"What does that prove, though?" he asked, puzzled. "What could it mean?"

"Well, for one thing, those two people had a child, and then all of a sudden she was gone!"

"But it proves *nothing*," he repeated. "What do

Sarah

you make of it? What do think it means?" he asked again.

"What I think, is that she was murdered and buried down in the basement," she blurted out, afraid of what he would think.

"I don't understand your logic," he muttered. "Maybe the kid went to live with her grandmother, somewhere. You said the dad was a mean devil; maybe the mother sent her away." He couldn't for the life of him figure out how his wife, seeing imaginary things in the basement, meant that someone had been murdered. He shook his head and smiled at her. They didn't talk about it anymore and went to bed.

He lay awake for a long time after Carol had gone to sleep. Finally he could stand it no more and got up out of bed. He crept out of the bedroom and started down the stairs, careful not to step on the fourth one where it squeaked. He turned on a light when he got to the kitchen and opened the basement door. He snapped on the light switch and started down the stairs, thinking he may be crazy, too. Well, he didn't really think his wife was crazy, but he sure didn't know what had gotten into her lately.

He got to the bottom of the steps and walked over to where the washer and dryer stood. He pulled the light string overhead and sat down on the chair that his wife sat on when she watched the phenomenon or whatever the hell it was. Then he waited and waited and waited - nothing happened. He saw nothing. He rubbed his jaw, folded his arms across his chest, and stared at the cement patch on the floor.

That's where Carol said the little girl stood each time she saw her. Still nothing.

He wasn't convinced, though, that his wife was imagining this. She was so serious when she told him about it and she certainly wasn't prone to fantasizing about anything. "She's a solid and sensible woman . . . I just don't understand," he murmured to no one.

He stood up and pulled on the light string. The basement was dark except for the light in the stairway. Standing still for a minute, he thought he should feel weird or something, but didn't. "Carol's private ghost," he whispered. "Oh, and the animals', too." He climbed the stairs and was surprised when he saw the clock in the kitchen. He had been sitting down there for forty-five minutes.

He went upstairs and got into bed; Carol didn't stir. She was sound asleep with Sophie wrapped around her legs. He lay awake for another half hour or so before finally falling asleep. He had some pretty strange dreams that night.

The next morning, Carol walked out to the car with him as he was leaving for work and startled him with what she said.

"You know, I really think that we should open that patch on the floor in the basement," she told him.

"What?" Doug asked with an incredulous look on his face.

"I said, I think we should open up that patch on the floor in the basement," she repeated, patiently.

"What for? Isn't the floor drain working?"

"Yes, Dear; the drain is working fine. I just want

to know what it is, that's all."

They kissed good-bye and he drove off, more puzzled than ever.

She had a hunch. No, it was more than a hunch, it was a strong feeling. She shook her head, no it wasn't even that. She felt *compelled* to find out what that cement patch was all about. She tried to carry on as normally as she could, knowing how confusing all this must be to her husband. He had never seen what she saw nearly every day now, and she was sure the kids had not. She thought it very curious that only she and the animals saw the girl.

~10~

The next day, Doug talked with Don over the hedge.

"Don, you know that business Carol told you about in our basement?"

"Yes, but she hasn't said much about it lately though. Why?"

"Well, she's got it in her head now that I should dig up that patch of cement down there."

"What for?" Don asked, frowning.

"I don't know for sure, but she's pretty darned insistent!"

"Well, you're not going to do it, are you, Doug?"

"I really don't think I have a choice, Don, she won't let it go. I wondered if you would help me."

"Well, sure I will, but I think it's silly. What does she think that has to do with what she sees, or should I say, thinks she sees?"

"I'm not sure, but maybe this will put an end to the whole thing."

"Well, I'm all for that. How did you plan to go about it?" Don wondered.

"I thought maybe I could chisel around the edge,"

Doug told him. "And then get under it with a crowbar. Do you have a crowbar, by chance?"

"Yes, I have two. Probably need the biggest one for cement. How big is it?" Doug showed him by measuring the air with his hands.

"Yeah, the big one should do it. Do you have a chisel? And a mallet? We'll need that, too."

"Yes, I have that," Doug said. "Just need the crowbar. I'll pick up a bag of cement so we can patch it up again. Is Saturday good for you? Say about nine o'clock?"

"Fine with me, neighbor."

"Thank you, Don. You don't know how much I appreciate it. This has been difficult for all of them. I hope this will put an end to it," Doug said, shaking his head.

"So do I, my friend. So do I," Don agreed.

Carol was pretty sure that she was on the right track. *If I'm not . . . well then, I don't want to think about that.* She would know Saturday. She tried to stress the importance of this to Doug, and how much she appreciated the fact that he was willing to do it. He still looked confused, but he was trying to help. She wondered what she would have done if he told her he'd seen a ghost by the washing machine, and thought that she probably wouldn't have been as good about it as he had been.

It really had been difficult for all of them, but especially Carol. It was hard for her to be herself now that she was seeing this phenomenon on a daily basis, but at least she felt she had a plan. She didn't feel so helpless.

~~~

It was Indian summer. They had frost a few nights before, and now it was hot again.

"This is the end of the season," Carol told the kids. "Now it's fall. My favorite time of year."

"Me too. Fall's my favorite, too," Troy agreed. "How come it's your favorite, Mom?"

"Well, the leaves are so pretty," she said. "And the days are cooler, except for Indian summer, and they're shorter, too. It gets dark early and we can spend a long time in the house before we have to go to bed. We can have a fire in the fireplace, watch television, play a game, or maybe just read. I love it."

"That's just why I like it," he said, agreeing with his mother. She smiled at him, knowing he'd never thought of it before.

"Mom!" Jennifer called from the front porch.

"I'm in the kitchen," Carol answered.

Jenny and Allison came through the hall. "Mom, we're so hot, we can't stand it! Can we have some soda?"

"Yes, or lemonade. We have both. Why don't you put your shorts on if you're so hot?" Carol suggested.

"Well, I don't want to because Allison can't, 'cause she doesn't want to go all the way home," Jenny explained.

"Well, let her wear a pair of yours. I'm sure they'll fit."

"Oh, I'm so stupid!" Jenny said, hitting her head with the palm of her hand. "Why didn't I think of that? Do you want soda or lemonade, Allison?"

"Soda, I guess," Allison said. Then she added, "I

didn't think of that either," defending her friend.

"Go up and change. I'll pour the soda," Carol told them.

"Thank you," both girls said in unison and ran through the hall and up the stairs.

"I want some, too," Troy told his mother. "With ice cubes in it."

"Yes, Sir! One soda with ice cubes, coming up!"

"You're funny, Mom," he said, grinning at her.

She did feel so much better. When we figure out this Sarah thing, we can get back to the business of normal living, she thought, as she poured everyone a cold drink. She heard the girls coming down the stairs a few minutes later, chattering and giggling together.

"They fit just perfect, Mom," Jenny said. "We're the same size! We're a lot alike, too, aren't we, Allison?" Her friend nodded in agreement.

"We like the same things, too!"

"Well, not everything," Allison said, and they giggled some more.

"I think I'll cook supper outside. It's too hot to turn on the oven today," Carol said.

"What are we having, Mom?" Jenny asked.

"I'm going to try roast beef on the grill. Does that sound good to you? I'm not sure how long it will take to cook, though. I want it done when Daddy gets home, so I think I'll light the grill now. I'll be right back. You girls should play on the back porch. Isn't it awfully hot out in front?" she asked the kids.

"No, it's shady on the porch. And besides we have all our junk out there," Jenny told her.

"When do you have to be home, Allison?" Carol

asked.

"By five o'clock," the girl replied.

"I'll watch the time for you."

"Thanks, Mom," Jenny said, as the two ran out to the front porch and crawled under the tent they had constructed out of an old sheet.

Two days until Saturday, Carol thought, as she lit the grill. It certainly is hot. Maybe I'll go downstairs to cool off while this heats up. She was going down there now as much as she could, trying to make it seem as though she were doing something that needed doing.

"Troy, the grill is hot now. Stay away from it, okay?"

"I will, Mom. Where you going?" he asked.

"I'll be back in a few minutes," she told him, not answering his question.

"Okay," he said, shoveling sand.

The basement was cool and quiet. She sat on the chair as she always did, and waited. In just a moment or two Sarah was there.

"Hello, Sarah," she whispered. The girl was very discernable today. Her hands were at her sides with the palms upwards. "I wish you could talk to me, Honey," she said to the figure that stood before her. "Well, I guess you do in a way, don't you? I'm doing the best I can for you, Sweetheart. Trust me!" The girl stayed a few more minutes and then simply vanished.

Oh, I'll be relieved when this is over, Carol thought, as she stood up and tapped the cement patch with her foot. She put all her weight on it and gave a little jump.

Sarah

"Certainly is solid," she muttered.

~~~

The grill was hot. She browned the roast on all sides and then put it in a pan on the top shelf, off to the side of the heat. Now, that should bake just like an oven, she thought. *I hope.* She went back into the house and got a meat thermometer.

"That should do it," she said.

"What did you say, Mom?" Troy was making roads in his sandbox.

"Nothing, Honey. I was talking to myself."

"I never talk to myself. I don't know what to say," he told her.

"Oh, I'll bet you do sometimes," She said, and sat on the porch steps. She sipped her soda and watched her son. Sadie was close beside him, watching what he was doing.

Carol was thinking about Sarah and wondering what had happened to her; she had a sense of something terrible, but no proof. She almost hoped they wouldn't find anything in the cellar because it couldn't be good, but she felt she had to know for Sarah's sake. Feeling more relaxed now than she had since they moved in, she was looking forward to Saturday, eager to learn what lay beneath that mysterious patch of cement that was taking over her every thought.

Sophie came out from underneath the porch, blinking in the sunlight.

"Oh, you found a cool place, didn't you, Soph'? Come here and I'll scratch your ears for you." The cat rubbed herself on Carol's legs and sat next to her on the step. They sat together enjoying the moment.

She had eaten lunch in the gazebo earlier, alone with a book. There wouldn't be many more days to do that sort of thing. She got up and checked the meat - so far so good. She had never cooked a roast this way before, but it looked and smelled good. She went into the kitchen and checked the time.

"Jennifer! Allison!" she called through the house. "Better start picking up your things. It's ten to five."

"Okay, Mom. We will."

~~~

Dinner tasted good; everyone said so. She would have to cook a roast like that again sometime. The kids carried their plates to the sink and rinsed them off before going out to play.

"What's the cement for, Dad?" Jenny asked, when she saw Doug take the bag out of the trunk of the car.

"I'm going to repair that patch in the basement floor - try to make it smoother, Jen," he lied.

"Oh, I see." There were no further questions. He was relieved. They had decided to say nothing to Jenny and Troy. They would wait and see what they found and go from there. Well, that was what Carol had said. He was pretty positive they wouldn't find a thing. What had happened to his sensible, stable wife, he wondered.

~11~

Carol was awake long before anyone else was on Saturday morning. She got up, put on her robe and crept down to the basement. It was barely light. She sat on the chair and waited. In a few minutes Sarah was there.

"Hi Sarah," she whispered. "It's Saturday, Honey. This is the day we're going to open up the floor where you're standing. Do you know what I'm saying to you? Do you even hear me? Do you understand me at all?" She knew very little about psychic phenomena, and now wished that she had taken time at the library to read about it. Sarah just stood there with her hands at her sides, as she always did.

Carol heard someone coming down from upstairs. She hoped the kids weren't up yet. It was much too early. Then she could tell by the footsteps in the kitchen that it was the dog. Sadie went down to the landing and looked between the stairs to see who was in the basement at this hour.

"Come on, girl," Carol called to her. "I didn't mean to wake you," she said, as the dog came down the steps. "Come sit by me. I'm talking to Sarah." Sadie's tail was wagging and she was looking at the girl. Then she sat down next to the chair and Carol began to stroke her. "Sadie sees you too, Sarah. At least I think she does, don't you, girl?" She put her head down to the dog and got a wet kiss on her cheek. They sat there quietly for a few minutes watching Sarah. Then she began to fade.

"Good-bye, Sarah Lorence," Carol said, softly, and the girl was gone. She had a feeling that she wouldn't see her again. She went up to the kitchen and made coffee.

"Come on, girl. I'm sure you need to go out." Sadie's ears perked up and she followed Carol to the back door. It was chilly today, but sunny and beautiful. When the coffee was done, she took a mug out to the back porch and sat on the step. Everything was still except for a few birds chirping in the trees. She sat quietly, watching the dog and contemplating all that had happened to her in this house.

~~~

When breakfast was over and everyone was dressed, Don walked over carrying his crowbar over his shoulder.

"Hi - ho, hi - ho, it's off to work I go," he was singing.

The kids were laughing at him. "Mom, did you hear Don?" Jenny asked. "He's singing the seven dwarfs' song! He's so funny!"

"Hi, Don. Come on in," Carol called from the pantry window. "Have you had coffee?"

"Not quite enough, Carol. Is it made?" he asked.

"Yes," she answered, pouring two big mugs full. "Doug will be down in a minute."

Don sipped his coffee and got the kids to giggling again as he sang some more.

"Morning, Don. You ready for this?" Doug asked, coming into the kitchen

Don nodded, he was ready.

"Is one of those for me, I hope?" Doug asked, pointing to the mugs of coffee.

"Yes, Dear," she said, handing him a mug. "I think I'll take the kids with me to the store. I just need a few things. That way, we'll be out of your way."

"Good idea," he said, kissing her on the cheek.

"Are you two ready to go?" she asked them.

"In a minute. Do we need a jacket?" Jenny asked.

"I think so, it's chilly. Get your red one. That will be warm enough, Jen. Troy, yours is in the dining room."

"Can we bring some money, Mom?" Troy asked.

"Do you have any?" she asked.

"A little," he said.

"Not from your piggy bank though, right?" she reminded him.

"Right. I'm saving that for something special," he said.

"Now I'm ready," Jenny said, coming into the kitchen.

"Do you have money, Jen?" asked Troy.

"No, do you?"

Troy nodded.

"I'll go get some; wait a sec'," Jenny said, running through the hall and back up the stairs.

"Mom says not from your piggy bank, though!" Troy yelled at his sister.

"I'll bet the neighbors heard that," Carol said, laughing. "Well, good luck, you guys," she said, as the two men started toward the basement door, armed with their tools and coffee.

"Thanks, Hon," Doug said, putting on a big smile for her.

"We won't be gone long. Thanks again, Don." she said, and they left for the store.

She wondered how long it would take and wished that she could stay and watch, but didn't want the kids there if . . . if what?

They walked to the store and took their time finding the things on the list that she had written the night before. The kids bought candy with their own money and ate it on the way home.

"You want a piece, Mom?" Jenny asked.

Carol was lost in thought.

"Mom! I said, do you want a piece?" she repeated.

"What? Oh, no thank you, Honey."

~~~

Meanwhile, the two men were in the basement.

"Well, how do you want to start?" Don asked, as they stood over the patch in the floor.

"I can't believe we're actually doing this. What if she still insists that there's something down here after we go through all this? Then what?" Doug said, sounding perturbed with the whole thing.

"Let's just get the darn thing opened up and worry about all that later," Don suggested.

"Right," Doug said, picking up the chisel. "I thought if I chiseled around the edge enough so we

Sarah

could get the crowbar in, we could use it like a lever. I've got this brick here for the fulcrum under the bar," Doug said. "What do you think?"

"Should work," Don said, laughing. "And you thought you'd never use what you learned in General Science, right? Do you have another chisel? It'll go faster if I help."

"Yeah, somewhere around here," Doug said, and went to the bench where his tools were kept. He returned to the patch, handing what was needed to his neighbor. "Here you go. Here's a hammer, too."

They got down on their knees and started.

"This has been here for over thirty years," Don said. "Got to be at least that long."

Both men had an ominous feeling as they chiseled around the edges of the patch, but neither said anything to the other. It was going pretty slow.

"Ah, now she's starting to go," Don said. "Yours, too?"

"Yes, it's coming," Doug answered. "It doesn't seem to be very thick - that helps. Let's try the crowbar. Hand me that brick will you, Don?" He placed the crowbar under the loosened edge of the patch and pushed it as hard as he could against the brick.

"No go," Don said, shaking his head. "Maybe if we break it up some we'll have better luck." They both worked on cracking the patch into large pieces.

"Try it again, Doug. I think it will move now." Slowly they were able to loosen and remove the chunks of cement.

"Nothing but earth. What a surprise!" Doug said, sounding relieved.

"Wait a minute. What's that?" Don asked, brushing dirt off something sort of gray. "What *is* that?" he asked a second time.

"I'll get a brush. If we clean it off, we can see it better," Doug said, and went back to his workbench.

Don had a strange feeling as he brushed away more dirt with his hand. It was pretty big, whatever it was.

"Here, this will help," Doug said, returning with a paintbrush. He was reminded of the digs in ancient Egypt that he had just seen on television as he brushed away the dirt.

"Holy Mary," Don whispered.

"Holy shit!" Doug exclaimed, unable to believe what he saw. It surely was a bone; a thigh bone, he thought. They both brushed and scraped and dug around until they could see that it was a small skeleton; a child, just like Carol had said.

"We'd better call someone about this, don't you think?" Don asked, nearly breathless.

"Who do you call?" Doug wondered. "God, I feel like such a jerk! I didn't believe her; I kept thinking she was hormonal or something."

Don put his hand on Doug's shoulder and got to his feet. "I think we call the coroner on something like this, Doug. You know, I didn't believe her either. In fact, I told her if she could just put it out of her mind, it would probably go away," he said, shaking his head. "We'll have to make it up to her, somehow," he added.

"I suppose we shouldn't mess around with it too much. They can do that - it's their job," Doug said.

"Right," Don said, staring at the what they had

just uncovered.

The skeleton was in a fetal position, on its right side. Part of the skull was broken and in pieces, with long strands of hair still attached.

"A little girl," one of the men whispered.

"Let's go upstairs and call the authorities," Don suggested. "Want me to do it for you, neighbor?" He thought Doug looked pretty shaken, more so than he was at the moment.

"That would be great. I appreciate it," Doug said, ashen faced.

~12~

Don and Doug were in the kitchen, talking quietly and waiting for the coroner to return their call, when Carol and the kids came home. She could tell by their faces that they had found something.

"Are you done already?" she asked.

"Yes. We're waiting for the coroner to call back," Doug said, as he went to her and took her in his arms. "There's a *skeleton* down there," he whispered in her ear. "Just like you said, under the cement patch. I'm so sorry I didn't believe you. I don't know what to say."

"Oh, I can't tell you how relieved I am. I thought I was losing my mind at times," she said.

"I'm sorry, too, Carol," Don said, putting his hand on her shoulder. "I thought you were imagining things. I'm really sorry."

Carol brushed away their apologies. "It's okay. I want to see her," she said, heading for the basement door. "The kids are out in back. Don't tell them anything, yet." She rushed down the stairs and knelt by the hole in the floor.

"Sarah. Oh, Sarah," she cried. "I knew you'd be

here; I just knew it! This is what you wanted, wasn't it? A proper burial and a place to rest. We'll do that for you, Sweetheart. I promise." She blew her nose and wiped away her tears.

"Who did this to you? It was him, wasn't it? Your own dad," she said, brushing more of the earth away with her hand. She heard the phone ringing, or was it just in her head? Things were spinning as she got up from the floor and sat on the chair where she always sat to watch the girl, but it was very different this time.

In a minute or two, Sophie came silently down the stairs and slowly walked to the hole in the floor. She inspected it carefully. Sniffing around the edges, then meowed softly and went to where Carol sat. She rubbed against Carol's legs and stared at the hole.

"That's her, Sophie. That's Sarah. Now people will believe what we saw, won't they?" she said, stroking the cat's back. Doug had made sure that Sadie was outside when he and Don were down in the basement. The dog wouldn't have been as delicate as the cat in her inspection of Sarah. That was for sure.

"Carol!" Doug called from the kitchen.

She didn't know how long she and the cat had been sitting there.

"The coroner's on his way. You'd better come up here."

She stood up, never taking her eyes off of the little girl in the hole. "Coming!" she called. "Come on, Sophie - let's go up." The cat raced ahead of Carol up the stairs, and waited for her on the top step.

"He'll be here any minute, now," Doug said, when she got to the kitchen.

"What are we going to tell him?" she asked. "Maybe we don't have to say that I saw her," she suggested, afraid of what people would think. "We could say that we were trying to find the floor drain or something . . . I don't know."

"Let's just wait and see what they ask us," Don offered.

"That's a good idea, but shouldn't we tell them what we know about the family?" Carol asked, rubbing her forehead. "I'm sure they would follow up on anything that we say."

"I think he's here. I saw a car stop out front," Doug said, walking through the hall to the front door. "Oh, geez! There's a cop car, too."

The coroner came up the walk, carrying a white box. He looked up and saw Doug in the doorway. "You the one who called?" he asked, as he climbed the stairs to the porch.

"Yes, sir, I am," Doug said, opening the door and extending his hand. "Well, actually my neighbor made the call, but this is my house. I'm Doug Benson."

"Jeff Grant, county coroner," the burly man said.

"Please come in," Doug said, holding the door for him. Carol and Don were waiting in the front hall. "This is my wife, Carol, and my neighbor, Don Hansen. Coroner Grant."

The coroner shifted the box he was carrying and shook hands with Don and nodded to Carol. "Now, what's this business about some remains in the cellar? You think they're human, do you?"

"Well, we know they are. Come see for yourself," Doug said, and led the way to the basement door. They all went down the stairs and stood over the remains of Sarah. It was then that Carol remembered the kids.

"Excuse me, please. I'm going to check on the kids," she said, and hurried up the stairs.

"Mom! There's a police car out in front and a black car with something written on it! What are they doing here?" Jenny wanted to know. Just then the sheriff's car arrived, too.

"Oh, Lord!" Carol muttered. "You kids come with me." She took them into the dining room and sat at the table with them. "Daddy and Don found some bones in the basement and we think they may be a person," she began, firmly believing in telling them the truth. "There's nothing for you to worry about, though. The bones have nothing to do with us, even though we live here. Do you understand?"

"How can there be bones down there. That means someone died," Jenny said, thoughtfully. "When people die, they go to the cemetery like Grandpa did, right? So how can that be?"

"Maybe it's just a dumb rabbit or something. Not a real person," Troy said, thinking that would be easier to have to think about.

"No, I don't think they're rabbit bones. I saw them," their mother told them.

By now the basement was full of people, or so it seemed. The coroner, the sheriff and his deputy, a policeman and Doug and Don were standing over the small skeleton. And now a few of their neighbors were beginning to congregate out in the front yard.

Carol wanted so badly to go downstairs, but she couldn't leave the kids.

"Is this why you were down the basement so much?" Jenny wanted to know, after thinking about it for a few minutes. "Did you know the bones were there? Did you, Mom?"

"Let's talk about it later, okay?" Carol said. "I think they're coming up, now."

She left the kids at the table and went into the kitchen. Doug was coming up the stairs.

"Oh, thank, God, it's you. What are they doing down there?"

"Removing the skeleton," he said. "They have to do an autopsy on it." He went to her and put his arms around her. He was overwhelmed with what was happening and was so sorry that he had doubted her.

She moved away from him and looked down the basement stairs. No one was coming up. "I thought they would do an autopsy," she said, quietly. "But how will they know for sure who she is? We know of no living relative for DNA testing, if that's possible," she said, running her fingers through her hair and biting her bottom lip.

"Go look out the front door," she told him. "There's a crowd gathering."

"You're kidding," he said, walking through the hall to the front of the house. She followed behind him and put her arms around his waist when he stopped at the door. She stood on her tip-toes and peering over his shoulder, watched the people in

Sarah

her yard.

"What do they want?" she asked, quietly.

"Oh, they just want to see what all the commotion is about, I guess," he answered. "Are the kids okay?" he asked. "What did you tell them?"

"They're in the dining room. I told them that you and Don found some bones in the basement and we think it may be a person. I told them we'd talk about it later. I don't want them to be afraid," she said.

They turned away from the front door and went through the living room and into the dining room.

"You kids doing all right?" Doug asked.

Carol went into the kitchen to get them something to drink.

"Did you really find somebody's bones, Dad?" Troy asked. Doug nodded.

"How do you know it's not a rabbit?" He was having trouble figuring out how a dead person could be in their basement.

"It's not a rabbit, Troy. You've seen people's bones in the encyclopedia, haven't you?"

"Yeah."

"Well, they don't look like a rabbit, do they, Buddy?"

"No, but how does a person get dead and get buried in somebody's basement, anyway?" he wondered. He just could not figure it out.

"I just want to know how you knew they were there?" Jenny said.

"Well, we didn't, really. Let's just wait and see what the coroner says when he comes up, okay?" Doug said.

"What's a corner?" Troy asked.

"It's *coroner* Troy. He's the guy who checks on this kind of thing. It's his job," Doug explained.

"Yuk! What a job! Who would want a job like that?" Jenny asked. Doug silently agreed, and went back to the front door.

"Oh, my God!" he whispered, exasperated by what he saw. "What the hell is this?"

Several of the neighbors were standing in groups talking quietly, and a van was pulling up to the curb. Channel WXXR News was written on the side.

"Oh, Jesus. You really started something here, Carol," he muttered. He went back to the kitchen just as the men were coming up from the cellar.

"Well, you were right," the coroner said. "These are indeed human remains; that of a child, I would say. A girl, I think. We'll be taking this back to our forensic lab for examination. We'll let you know what we find. Say, how long have you folks lived here?" he asked, as he rested the white box containing Sarah on the back of a kitchen chair.

"Just about two months," Doug answered. He noticed that the sheriff made a note of that.

"We may have some questions for you later. Okay if we give you a call?" asked the sheriff.

"Well, of course it's okay!" he said, looking around for his wife. Where the hell was she. Geez, did they think we had something to do with this? "Carol!" he called.

She settled Jenny and Troy in front of the television set with a snack and some juice. She told them that when everyone was gone, she and Daddy would explain this as best they could. They were content with that, so she went into the kitchen where the men were gathered. She saw the white box in the coroner's arms and a chill went up her spine. She walked over to where her husband stood and felt his arm go around her.

"Are you all set, then?" she asked.

"Just wondered why you decided to dig up that spot down there?" the deputy asked. "Just curious, you understand."

"Well, it was my idea, actually," Carol said. "I *sensed* something."

"You sensed something?" the deputy repeated and looked at the sheriff.

"Yes, that's right. I sensed something," she said.

Oh boy, Doug thought, here it comes.

"I've done a little investigating, too, and I think I may know who she is," she told them. They all looked at her, wondering what she meant by that.

The sheriff's deputy thought that she must be a real piece of work, as he liked to say. He hated when people tried to do their own investigating. It wasn't, after all, their job. It was his and the sheriff's. "Is that so?" he asked her, smugly, looking at the other men.

"Would it be okay if I come back later after I fill out the paper work on this?" the coroner asked, nodding to the white box. "We can talk about it then," he said, trying to smooth over the attitude of the deputy.

"That will be fine," Carol said, as they all walked through the hall to the front door. Sadie was sitting looking out the screen door at all the activity in the yard. Sophie was on the back of the couch, looking out through the window. She wasn't about to be as near to whatever was going on out there as that stupid dog was. She could, at any moment, jump down behind the couch and hide if she felt the need.

"Sadie, move please," Carol said. The dog obeyed and went into the living room. They didn't expect what they saw in the yard. There were more people now than there were the last time they had looked out, and a television camera was filming them coming out of the house.

A woman with a microphone approached the coroner and the cameraman zoomed in on the white box he was carrying.

"What can you tell us, Coroner Grant?" the woman asked. "We're anxious to know what's in that box. Talk right into the microphone and look at the camera, if you would, please."

"Well, it seems, these people have found some human remains down in the cellar in the house. We will examine what we have here and do a thorough investigation. That's all. Thank you," he said, and walked around her to his car before she could ask anything more.

By now the kids were out, too. They weren't sure what was going on, but were fascinated by the idea of maybe being on television and were talking freely to the woman with the microphone.

"No, we didn't know about the bones, but we think our mom did," Troy told her, proudly. Carol heard that and ran to where they stood talking.

"Please don't," she pleaded with the woman. "They know nothing about this." She looked up and saw the cameraman filming them. She smiled and turned away with her children.

"Mom, I think I saw Allison!" Jenny exclaimed. "It is her," she cried, waving to her friend. Jenny ran to meet her. She couldn't wait to tell her what was happening. Troy was close behind, trying to get to Allison first with the people bones story.

Debbie was there with Cassy draped over her arm. She waved her arm over her head so Carol would see her. "Carol! Is it true?" she yelled. "You found a skeleton in the basement and you saw its ghost? God, I would just freak!" They were closer now so she lowered her voice. "How can you be so calm, Carol?"

"Who told you that?" Carol wanted to know.

"Everyone's talking about it. Why didn't you tell me. I've never seen anything like that in my life. I wish you would have told me," she whined.

That was all that Carol could take. "Will you excuse me, Debbie?" she asked, politely. "I think I'll go inside."

"Oh, sure, go ahead. I don't blame you. God, you are so calm!" she said again.

"Bye, Cassy," Carol said, rubbing the baby's soft little face with the back of her hand. She climbed the porch steps as she looked over the yard for the kids. They were standing with Doug - they were okay.

It was a relief to be inside again. Sadie was sitting in the middle of the living room, wagging her tail, and the cat was still on her safe perch. They raised their faces to her as though they were waiting for some explanation for the chaos outside.

"Come here, you two," she said, leading the way to the stairway. "Come sit with me for a minute." There they sat, the three of them, together on the steps.

"We're the only ones who know what happened here, aren't we?" she said, nuzzling them both. "And you never thought I was crazy, did you? You saw Sarah, too, didn't you?" She put her head in her hands to block out the activity outside, when the screen door opened. It was the woman with the microphone.

"I'm Angie Cromwell from Channel Six," she said. "Would you like to make a statement? It will be on the five o'clock news."

Carol told her that she was glad it was over, but thought she might miss her.

"Oh, so then it's true? You did experience some clairvoyance? I heard them talking about that outside, but I'd like to hear it from you," she said.

"I'm not even sure if I know what that means," Carol told her. "I don't think I've been much help. I really don't want to talk about it, I'm sorry. This has been hard on all of us, hasn't it?" she said, putting her head down to her furry friends.

"You did just fine," Angie said. "Be sure and watch the news tonight. Your whole family will be on!" She started out the door, then stopped. She turned back to Carol and asked. "How did you manage to get matching animals?"

"We had them re-upholstered," Carol said, laughing.

~~~

The activity in the yard ended. Most of the neighbors had returned to their homes. A few stragglers remained, hoping to hear more about the sensational find in the cellar.

~13~

"I'm glad that's over," Carol said, as she huddled with her family in the living room. "It's almost time for lunch. Are you kids hungry?" They were, as usual. What a morning it had been. She was sure the kids would be full of questions.

They ate lunch together at the kitchen table and answered the questions as best they could. It wasn't easy, as there was much she didn't understand herself. She didn't mention actually *seeing* Sarah, but explained that she had a strong feeling that something was under the cement patch in the floor and that Daddy said he would look for her.

"It was kind of rough, anyway," Doug explained. "After lunch I'm going to patch it up again. Maybe I can get it real nice and smooth."

"Do you think you should do that?" Carol asked. "What if they come back and want to look again."

"The coroner told me I could. They're done down there," he told her.

She nodded and finished her lunch.

"I could help you, Dad," Troy said. "I think I know just how to make cement."

Sarah

"You do?" Doug asked.

"Yup, I do."

"Well, that's settled then. I could use some help."

Carol thought that maybe someday she would tell them about what she saw, but didn't think it would be a good idea just now. A ghostly figure in their own basement might frighten them. She hoped the neighborhood kids would soon forget about it. If not, she probably could explain it to Jenny. She was sure that she and Allison would talk at length about it. She pushed back her chair and stood.

"Why don't you guys go down and start fixing that hole," she suggested. "I'll clean up here."

"Mom, can I go to Allison's? Please," Jenny pleaded.

"Why don't you call and see if she can come here today," her mother said.

"You don't mind? After all that happened?" she asked.

"No, I don't mind," she said, thinking it would be better if they were here. Less people to talk with about what happened, she reasoned.

~~~

The coroner returned at four o'clock that afternoon. Doug and Carol answered his questions and tried to explain what had transpired since they moved into the house. Carol did most of the talking, as she was the only one who could. He listened intently and didn't interrupt her. When she was finished he smiled and shook his head.

"I'm not here to judge you, Mrs. Benson, and I must admit that I don't put much stock in this sort of thing, but you tell a very convincing story. I don't know how you would have known about the remains if what you say isn't true," he told her, seriously. "I have never encountered anything like this in all my years as coroner. It is puzzling, indeed."

They talked more and the coroner told them that there would be an investigation into the matter and that they would receive a letter in the mail as to the findings. "Because the remains were found in the house that you own," he explained. "Or should I say, the house that you and the mortgage company own," he said, laughing, knowing they had only lived there a short time.

"Well, that would be more like it," Doug said, laughing along with him. They walked him out to the porch and watched him drive away.

"I'm certainly glad that he came back to question us and not the sheriff's deputy," Carol said, not liking the way he had spoken to her earlier. They closed the door on the world and welcomed the privacy of their home.

"We can't forget to watch the news, kids!" Doug reminded them.

"We won't, Dad," they said together. Allison had gone home, so they were alone now.

"How does spaghetti sound to everyone for dinner?" Carol asked.

"That's fine, Hon," Doug said.

"Good, Mom," Troy called from the living room.

"Will it take long?" Jenny wondered. "I'm starving!"

"No. We'll eat soon; after the news is on," Carol said.

Whenever she made meatballs, she would make

Sarah

extra and keep those in the freezer for future meals. It made spaghetti and meatballs an easy supper. She put the water on the stove to boil and prepared a salad.

"I'm thirsty, Mom," Troy said, coming out to the kitchen.

"Well, have a drink of water. We'll be eating soon," she told him.

He watched her measure, in her hand, the amount of spaghetti she would need.

"You know what, Mom?" he asked.

"No. What, Troy?"

"You know Jason's dad?"

"Yes, I know who he is. Why?" Conversations with her son were usually quite lengthy.

"Well, when he makes spaghetti, ya know?" he asked, waiting for her to respond.

"Yes," she answered.

"Well, he throws it at the wall to see if it's done!" he told her, watching for her reaction.

"No!" she said, sounding astonished.

"Yes, it's true. Jason told me so, and I saw him do it the last time I ate over there," he said. "I think if it sticks on the wall . . . um . . . I think it's done, but I'm not sure."

She smiled and salted the water. "I think I'll check it the way I always do, if it's okay with you," she said.

"Mom! The news is almost on," Jenny called from the living room.

She turned down the flame under the water and went to join them. It was the lead story on the five o'clock news. How odd it was to see their house on television.

"There I am!" Troy cried. "Jenny, there you are, too!"

"Oh, my hair looks funny," Jenny said. Her parents looked at each other and rolled their eyes.

They listened quietly to what Angie Cromwell was saying. ". . . it looks as though this little girl came to a violent end; possibly at the hands of someone close to her. We'll know more after an autopsy is done and the case is investigated," she said, as the camera panned the front of their house. Thank goodness, she had not mentioned anything about Carol seeing the girl.

"Well, I think we're a pretty darn good-looking family, if I say so myself," Doug said when the report ended. "Let's eat!"

"It will be ready in a few minutes," Carol told them. "Go wash your hands."

"I'm going to check the cement in the basement. It might be dry," Doug said, and headed downstairs.

Carol thought about how different it would be now when she went down to do the laundry. She felt a little sad, because she had gotten so used to seeing Sarah every day, but mostly she was relieved. For one thing, she wasn't losing her mind, and for another, she had taken care of the problem as well; she felt good about that.

They ate piles of spaghetti and talked more about the little girl named Sarah. Jenny wondered who had put the girl down there.

"If someone has an accident, don't you take them to a hospital or a doctor, or *something*? You don't just put them in the basement, do you?" she asked.

Sarah

"Can if you want," Troy said, between sucking single strands of pasta into his mouth.

"Well, no you can't, Troy," his dad explained, looking at his wife for help. How could they explain this? Especially to their kids, who wouldn't dream that parents could hurt their own child.

"Some people aren't very nice," she began, hesitantly. "It's very hard to understand that, but it's true. Sometimes parents hurt their own children," she said, watching them carefully. "But not very often, thank goodness."

Jenny stared wide-eyed at her mother. "Do you think that Sarah's mom or dad hit her and hurt her?" she asked.

"Well, we don't know for sure, but it's looks as though someone hurt her. Maybe pushed her down the stairs," she told them.

"That's mean," Troy said, licking pasta sauce from his fingers. "Who would do that?"

"We don't know, but someone hurt her bad," Doug said. "We'll know more when we get the letter from the coroner." Thinking that they had heard enough truth for one day, the subject was changed.

~~~

And then the phone started to ring . . . .

"Well, yes, that's true, but don't believe everything you hear!" Doug said. "Thank you for your concern," he added. "Good-bye."

"That's the fifth call in half an hour!" Carol said, exasperated by the intrusion. "Maybe we should leave it off the hook." And then it rang again.

"Mom!" Jenny called from upstairs. "It's for you. Mrs. Lester wants to talk to you."

"Okay, Jen. I've got it." Carol planned to call the woman after the news report, but it had slipped her mind. She knew that if Mrs. Lester watched the report on television, she would certainly be curious about what was happening in the house where she had lived for so long.

"Hello, Mrs. Lester. I'm fine, thank you, and you?" she spoke softly into the phone. "I was going to call you. Did you see it on television?" she asked. "Yes, I thought you may have." They talked for several minutes. Carol left out the part about seeing Sarah and told her that they wanted to replace the irregular patch with a smoother surface. She hated lying, but thought it would be a bit much for the elderly woman to think she'd had a spirit in the basement all the while she had lived there.

"I bet you a dollar, Carol, that it was Clyde who did it! I told you he was mean, but this is horrible. I must say, I'm shocked," Edith Lester said.

"Well, we don't know anything for sure, but they said that a copy of the report would be mailed to us. We'll know more then," Carol told her.

"Well, from what Don told us about him, I wouldn't put it past him," Edith continued, with anger in her voice. "I wish he were still alive, so they could lock him up."

"Well, if he did it, Edith, he got away with it. I'm sorry to say." They talked for a few more minutes and promised to keep in touch.

The next morning, a picture of their house was on the front page of the newspaper, along with an article telling all about how a skeleton was discovered in the cellar of the old house. All day long, cars would drive by and slow down in front of the house. Some even drove through the alley, hoping to catch a glimpse of something. Of what, Carol wondered, becoming annoyed with all of it.

She was surprised at how the kids had taken the discovery. They seemed to accept what had happened in their home. Oh, they were curious, and asked a lot of questions, but it didn't seem to have an adverse affect on either one of them. They had even taken their friends down to the basement to see the cement patch. Carol was happy that they hadn't seen the little girl, or the remains, as she had. She was sure it would have frightened them.

In a week or so, the story died down. They received an occasional phone call, and once in a while a car would drive slowly by the house, but for the most part it was over. The Bensons were grateful.

~~~

The report arrived in a very official looking envelope four weeks later. The autopsy revealed that the girl had suffered a crushing wound to the head, which fractured her skull, and a broken neck, which had caused her death. Her pelvis and right humerus were fractured as well. The letter stated that the Lorence family had been researched and no living relatives were found. After all avenues were exhausted, it was determined that the remains found in the cellar at 409 North Elm Street in Woodland Village, were that of one Sarah Mary Lorence, and would be laid to rest in the cemetery therein.

"My God, Sarah," Carol breathed, after reading the report over and over again. "I think he actually threw you down the stairs, didn't he?" she whispered. She was crying now and couldn't stop. The case was closed. There was no one to prosecute, the sheriff had said. It was over.

Carol was glad that Inez was gone now, too. Surely she would have been questioned and made to relive the horror of that night. She blew her nose, dried her tears and hoped that mother and daughter were together now, in a better place. Sarah was buried in an unmarked grave in the part of the small cemetery known as potter's field.

~14~

Life on North Elm Street was back to normal and plans were being made for their first Christmas in the house. Everyone was excited; especially the kids. Doug told them that he could run an electric cord out to the gazebo and put Christmas lights all around it.

"No one has Christmas lights in their *backyards*, Dad," Jenny said. "That will be so cool!"

"We can have a bigger tree this year, too," Carol told them. "And you can hang your stockings on the fireplace."

"I think Santa should still come through the front door like he did at our old house, though," Troy said.

"Why is that?" his mother asked.

"Because it's easier - did you ever look up that chimening? It's awful little," he said, thoughtfully. "Awful dirty, too," he added.

"I think we'll leave that up to Santa, okay?" Carol said.

"Okay. But I betcha he comes in the door," he muttered.

The shopping began. Each parent helped the kids find something for the other. They had many gifts to buy. Mom, Dad, Sadie, Sophie, each other and Grandma and Grandpa Benson. They wouldn't be seeing their grandparents this year, but they would mail them their gifts early so they would be sure to get them by Christmas.

~~~

"I think Mom would love this," Jenny told Doug, as she held up a pretty scarf and looked for the price tag. It was Saturday and he was helping them shop for Carol.

"It sure would look nice with her coat, Jen. How much is it?" he asked. The price was right, but she didn't want to buy the first thing she saw.

Troy found a bracelet that he liked. Just costume jewelry, of course, but very pretty, with pale blue crystals. "I'm gettin' this, for sure," he announced. "How much does it cost?" he asked his dad. He could afford it if his dad pitched in and helped with a few extra dollars. They looked around a bit more for what Jenny wanted to buy, and then decided on the scarf that she had seen first.

"I think that's a good choice, Jen," Doug told her. "Like I said before, it will look nice with her winter coat and it will keep her neck warm."

"Okay. I'll take this, please," she said, handing the scarf to the sales clerk.

"Do you want a gift receipt?" the woman asked.

Not sure what that meant, Jenny looked at Doug. He nodded and smiled.

"Yes, please," she answered.

"On to the pet shop," Doug said, and led them

out of the store and into the mall.

"Can we get a pretzel, Dad?" Troy asked.

"Let's get our shopping done first, okay? Then we'll get something," he said.

"I wish Sophie would wear a collar," Jenny said, as she looked at the small colorful collars for cats in the pet store.

"Well, you know she won't, so there's no point wasting your money, Jen," Doug told her. They bought a collar for the cat when they first got her, but Sophie had walked backwards, trying to get her head out of it until they took it off of her. A small mouse, stuffed with cat-nip was chosen instead. A rawhide bone for Sadie, and they were finished.

"I'm thinking about ice cream, now, not a pretzel," Troy said, as they gathered up their packages. They found a vacant table in the food court in the middle of the mall and told Doug what they wanted. Troy had changed his mind again and ordered a chocolate malt and was now noisily sucking the very last drop of it up the straw.

"I think it's gone, Buddy," Doug said, and moved the malt container away from his son.

"You are so gross, sometimes, Troy," Jenny said, as she daintily ate the last bit of her ice cream cone.

These two are as different as the cat and dog are, Doug thought, smiling as he watched his kids. "Everybody ready?" he asked. "Let's go home. Don't let Mom see the presents you bought for her."

"I'm hiding mine under my bed. She never looks there, " Troy told him. It had never occurred to him that his mother cleaned under there, too.

~~~

"No fair peeking," Troy announced when they entered the kitchen.

"I promise," Carol told him. "Next Saturday I'll take you shopping for Daddy, okay?"

"Okay," both kids said.

"You know, I've been thinking about something and I want to know what you two think," she said.

"What, Mom?" Jenny asked, curiously.

"I think that Sarah should have a stone on her grave. What do you think?"

"You mean like Grandma and Grandpa?"

"Well, not that big, Jen, but yes, a gravestone with her name on it."

"I bet they cost a lot," Jenny thought, aloud. "But I have my piggy bank money!"

"Remember how interested everyone was when we found Sarah in the basement?" their mother asked.

"Yes."

"Yeah."

"Well, I was thinking, maybe we could ask at the grocery store if we could put a can there for donations from all our neighbors. We could make a nice sign, too. Do you think it's a good idea?"

"What kinda sign?" Troy wondered.

"I think it's a good idea, Mom. I know Allison would help us, too," Jenny said.

"What kinda sign?" he repeated.

"Oh, maybe we could write, A STONE FOR SARAH, in big colored letters, and have a coffee can there with a slot in the top for money," Carol told them. "I'll bet that nice lady from the newspaper would write a bit in the paper for us, too."

"That would be cool, Mom!" Jenny exclaimed.

"What kinda stone?" Troy asked, sounding like a broken record.

"I don't know what kind, Troy. We won't know that until we see how much money we collect."

Carol felt good about this project and happy that her kids were willing to take money out of their banks for the cause; she was proud of them. She thought that being buried in potter's field was sad enough, and maybe a stone would make it better, somehow.

The next time she went shopping, she asked the manager at the grocery store if they could put up a sign. He thought it was a very nice gesture, especially at this time of year and he would be happy to oblige. Their plan was taking shape, nicely. A small article was written up in the paper and a colorful sign was made by Jennifer, Allison and Troy. The sign was in the window of the grocery store and coffee cans, covered with white paper, were at each checkout counter. The kids had drawn pictures on these and written Sarah in bold letters.

When Saturday came, they went shopping for Doug. Jenny wished that he smoked a pipe, because she liked the smell of tobacco and thought it would be a nice gift. Carol was secretly glad that he didn't. Troy found some monogrammed handkerchiefs for him, and Jenny picked a tie that would go nicely with his new suit.

"You know, I think we've forgotten someone," Carol said, as they were leaving the store.

"Who?" they asked.

"Our best neighbor, Don." she told them.

"You're right, Mom. We can't forget him," Jenny

said, and back into the store they went. They found some nice woolen gloves for him and guessed what size he would wear. The kids were finished with their shopping. Carol rather wished that she was, too.

~~~

The response to the fund raiser was unbelievable. The coffee cans were full in no time at all. It seemed that everyone wanted the little girl to have a marker on her grave, and at this rate they could have it by Christmas. The kids were excited, too, and gave generously from their savings. The week before Thanksgiving, Carol and the kids collected the money and drove into town to order the marker. Allison went, too, as she had helped with the sign painting and was truly interested in the project. They all thought that something simple would be best and found exactly that. It would be ready in about four weeks.

"That will be just perfect," Carol told the kids when they were in the car, going home. "Sarah will have her grave marker for Christmas. And now," she told them, "we must plan for Thanksgiving! We'll have a feast."

Every holiday took on special meaning now that they were in their own home. It was wonderful and they all worked together to make it nice.

The following Thursday, Carol was up early to get things started for dinner. Soon the house was filled with the aroma of pumpkin pie. She was taking it out of the oven when the others came straggling into the kitchen.

"Morning, Hon," Doug said, giving her a kiss and

heading for the coffee pot. "I didn't hear you get up. Looks like you've got a lot done."

"Not really. Just the pie. I want to get the turkey in soon. We should be eating around one o'clock. Sound okay to you?" she asked.

"Sounds great; we'll all help you, too," he told her.

"Oh, I'm counting on that!" she said, smiling.

"It smells good, Mom," Jenny said, yawning. "Want me to peel potatoes?"

"Sure, but not just yet. We have to have breakfast and get dressed first," she said, pulling the bag of giblets out of the turkey."

"What the heck is that stuff?" Troy said, as he watched his mother. "I'm not eatin' that junk!"

"You don't have to eat this, junk, as you call it, but I know someone who will."

Sophie was sitting at Carol's feet, head up, hoping for a morsel to drop her way.

"I'll cook this for you, Sophie," she said, hating the idea of eating it raw.

"She's just a cat, you know," Doug reminded her, reaching past her to get bowls for cereal.

"I beg your pardon! *Just a cat*? Did you hear that, Sophie?" she said, teasing. "I'll cook these parts and Sadie can have some, too. I'll mix it in with her food. It's Thanksgiving for them, too, you know."

He just shook his head and poured cereal for the kids. Those two animals had become a part of the family. He wasn't sure when that had happened - he thought they were just pets.

The meal turned out perfectly and everyone had

their fill, including the animals who were now having a nap. Carol smiled as she cleared the table and watched the two sleeping beauties. "You really have it rough," she said, quietly. They had eaten in the dining room, something they reserved for special occasions, and today was one for sure. She was grateful for many things this year; they had talked about it at dinner. The kids were thankful, too, especially for their new home and their very own bedrooms.

Doug and the kids were in the pantry scraping plates and starting to wash things. They were chattering excitedly about the next holiday.

"How far away is it now, Dad?" Troy asked, as he did every day.

Doug told him as he dried his hands. "Here's what we'll do," he said, pointing to the calendar. "Here's Christmas. See? Okay, we'll cross off every day, so you'll know how many more days until then," he told him, as he attached a string to a black marker and put it on the nail where the calendar hung. "Now cross off Thursday, the 23rd." Troy did as he was told.

"I sure hope I can remember to do it each day."

"Oh, I think you will," Doug said, laughing.

"What a good idea!" Carol said, as she brought more dishes into the pantry. She winked at her husband. Maybe now their son wouldn't ask them *every day*. "Maybe we started shopping too early," Carol whispered to Doug.

~15~

Two weeks later, the house was decorated and the tree was in the living room. They could wait no longer. Almost every night, after supper, they would light a fire in the fireplace and turn off the lights - all but the tree lights and candles. Sometimes they would roast marshmallows in the fire and once they made popcorn.

Out in the backyard, the gazebo was decorated with tiny white twinkle lights.

The kids had chosen white lights for out there and colored ones for the tree inside the house. Carol never remembered having this much fun when she was a little kid. It seemed that her mother was busier than ever at church around Christmas time. They always had a tree, of course (although the minute it dropped a needle, it was taken down) but they never really had fun. She wanted that for her kids; it seemed important to her. It was also important to her that they remember what Christmas was all about; the true meaning of the holiday. They talked about it one afternoon as they made Christmas cookies. They were out of school, now, until the new year.

"I think we'll go to the church on Walnut Street Christmas Eve. I heard that they have a candlelight service. Would you like that?" she asked them.

"What's a candlelight service?" Jenny wanted to know.

"Well, I don't think they use real candles because it would be too dangerous. Probably they use flashlights."

"Then it's a flashlight service," Troy said, popping a pecan into his mouth.

"No, it's not, dummy," Jenny said. "But what do they do with the lights?"

"Jenny, set the timer for ten minutes, will you please?" her mother asked. "Now, about the candlelight service. I'm not sure what they do here, but when I was a little girl, at our church, all the kids dressed in choir robes and carried a flashlight that looked like a candle. We walked around the church with our lights and sang Christmas Carols. The church was dark except for the tree lights and our candlelights. It was very pretty, as I remember."

"That sounds nice, Mom. I think we should go," Jenny said. "What time does it start?" she wondered.

"I think it starts pretty late, but we don't have to get up early in the morning, so it won't matter," Carol told them. "It's important to remember that Christmas is a very special birthday. All the other things are fun, but that's what it's really about. We'll read the story again, too, like we do every year."

Sarah

DING, went the timer. The cookies were done, and the kitchen smelled so good. "We'll taste them when they cool off a bit," their mother told them. "We'll make another kind next time; maybe tomorrow."

Troy was bored with the cookie baking and had gone into the living room to watch television, but Jenny didn't want to stop just yet.

"Can't we make some more, Mom?" she asked.

"It's getting late, Jen, I have to get supper soon, too."

"But I like to bake. It's fun."

"We could mix up a batch of dough and put it in the fridge to bake tomorrow," Carol suggested.

"Okay, which kind?" They chose a sugar cookie that could be cut out. "I'll measure for you, Mom," Jenny said. She was learning and having fun at the same time.

"I hope I can find my cookie cutters," Carol muttered, as they measured and mixed ingredients together. "If you sift the flour, Jen, I'll try to find them." Where had she put them? Kitchen things that she didn't use often . . . hmmm. "Oh, I remember. They're on the shelf in the basement. I'll get them," she said and went downstairs.

It still felt strange going down there, now. The cement patch was covered with an old rug, and Sadie, like Edith Lester's dog, liked to sleep there when Carol did laundry. She found what she was looking for and started up the stairs, when the phone rang.

"Can you get that, Jen?" she called.

"Mom, it's for you!" It was the Hudson Monument Company. The gravestone that they ordered was completed and would be in place after noon the following day.

"Sarah's stone is ready, kids," she called after she hung up the phone. "Tomorrow afternoon, if it's not too cold, we'll take Sadie and walk to the cemetery. We can drive if it's cold. I hope it looks nice!" she said, excitedly.

The following afternoon they were getting ready to leave for the cemetery. It was cold, but the sun was shinning and they were bundled up in warm jackets.

"I think we'll be warm enough, don't you?" Carol asked, as they left the house.

"It's not cold, Mom," Troy called, running ahead of the others. "The sun is out!"

He'd never understood that in the dead of winter, even though the sun was shining, it could be bone-chilling. She thought it was good for all of them, including the dog, to walk if they could.

The cemetery was about four blocks from home, right behind the church. It was very old. They walked through the big iron gates and instinctively lowered their voices.

"That one says, 1894," Jenny said, softly, pointing to one of the gravestones.

"This cemetery is very old," Carol told them. "See how some of the stones are crumbling?"

"Where's Sarah?" Troy asked.

"We have to walk way back to the end of the cemetery," their mother told them. "She's buried where people who have no families or no money are buried."

"We gave money for her," Troy said, rather indignantly.

"I know, Dear, but it was just enough for a marker. People who have families usually have a service and are buried with other people in the family. Do you remember Grandpa's funeral?"

"Sorta," he mumbled.

"Here we are," she said, as they reached the back of the cemetery where the graves were mostly unmarked, except for a cross or two. She saw the small mound of fresh earth. "I think that's it, " she said, pointing ahead.

Jenny ran ahead and shouted back to them. "It's Sarah!" Then realizing she was much too loud, covered her mouth in apology.

The others caught up with Jenny and stood over the grave.

"I like it," Carol said, quietly. "It really turned out nice."

"It's just what we wanted, right, Mom?" Jenny asked. Her mother nodded.

"Yeah, it's good," Troy mumbled.

It was a flat, oval, bronze marker, and it read, simply, SARAH.

"I think we'll come back one more time," Carol said. "We'll put some Christmas greens on Sarah's grave."

They walked slowly back to the gate, reading headstones aloud as they went. They all felt good about what they had done for the little girl found buried under the cement in their basement. Sadie was sniffing and inspecting the plantings around the graves as she walked. When they passed through the iron gate, they started running. Carol had to hold the leash when they ran, as Sadie was too fast for the kids. When they got to the corner, they slowed down to watch for cars. They were breathless.

"I think we'll just walk the rest of the way, okay?" their mother suggested.

"Oh, Mom, we want to run!" Jenny said.

"Well, you two go ahead; Sadie and I will walk. Stop at the next corner and wait for us." Off they went. Sadie seemed content to walk behind with Carol.

~16~

It was December 23rd, and they were ready. The shopping was done, the cookies were baked, and the house looked festive. They were eager for the next day, when the celebrating would begin. For a special treat, they had supper at a restaurant and went to a Walt Disney movie after. The kids had a good time and after a bath, went to bed willingly.

"The sooner you go to bed - the sooner the next day comes," Troy announced, as Doug helped him dry his hair.

"That's right, Buddy. I like your logic," his dad told him, hoping that he wouldn't have to define the word, logic. It went unnoticed by his son who was now concentrating hard on the job of putting toothpaste on his toothbrush. He liked to completely cover the bristles of his brush with the gooey stuff. No more. No less.

~~~

They were up early the next day, and Troy crossed off the last day on the calendar. It had finally arrived. They planned to go to the candlelight service at church later in the evening, but tomorrow was the big day. Don was coming, too. His daughter took her kids skiing, so he would be alone.

"You can't spend Christmas Day alone. It's not right. We'd love to have you!" Carol had told him. He was delighted.

But today belonged to them.

"I think we'll go to Sarah's grave today and put some Christmas greens on it," Carol told them after breakfast.

"Like what? What are greens?" Jenny wanted to know.

"We can cut some small branches from the back of our tree and tie them in a red bow. We can dig them into the ground or just lay them on top, next to the marker," she said.

"Okay. Should we walk again today?" Jenny wondered.

"I don't know, yet. Let's wait and see," her mother told her.

They chose to drive to the cemetery and took the dog along. The sky was gray and looked very much like it could snow. Jenny sat in the front seat, carefully holding the Christmas bouquet in her lap. Troy was in back with Sadie. They drove through the iron gates and slowly made their way to the back of the cemetery. Sadie was the first one out of the car. She ran right to Sarah's grave, surprising them all.

"How does she know which one it is?" Jenny wondered.

"She must remember from when we were here before," Carol told her, not sure if it was memory or some sense that the dog had.

"She's a smart dog," Troy stated.

Carol laid the evergreens on the grave next to the bronze marker and looked down in silence for a moment or two. The kids were quiet, too. Even the dog stood still. It seemed that all four of them were paying respect to the little girl they had discovered in the cellar.

"This is probably the last time we will come to see you, Sarah," Carol said. "We know you are resting now, in peace, and we're happy that we were able to help you."

"You did most of it, Mom," Jenny said, looking up at her mother. "We didn't do very much."

"Oh, but you did! You kids made the signs, gave money and . . ."

"Yeah, Jen, we did lots," Troy said.

They were walking back to the car when Sadie suddenly turned and raced back to the grave. She got down on her front paws, gave one loud bark and then ran to catch up with them.

"I think Sadie was saying good-bye to Sarah, too," their mother said.

~~~

The day had flown by and at 8:45 P.M. they were dressed in their Sunday best and ready to leave for the candlelight service. It was beginning to snow and huge fluffy lazy flakes landed on their heads as they walked to the car. A perfect Christmas Eve, Carol thought.

The service was beautiful and reminded Carol of her own church when she was young. The children were dressed in robes, as she had been, and carried small lights.

When the children were seated, the minister gave a short sermon and read the Christmas story from the book of Luke. Jenny was in awe and hoped very much to be a part of this next year. The organ music was pretty, too, and they all joined in and sang Silent Night at the end of the service. It was very moving.

As they were leaving the church, after the service, several people came up and introduced themselves. It was a very friendly parish and they were made to feel welcome.

The snow continued and was now showing on the ground.

"Just in time for Santa," Doug said, when they were in the car and heading for home.

"It's so beautiful," Carol murmured. "And so was the service. Did you like it?"

They all said that they did.

"I think I'd like to do that next Christmas," Jenny said.

"Maybe you can, Jen. We'll see," her mother told her.

When they arrived home, they turned on the tree lights and left the drapes open. It was indeed a beautiful, silent night.

"I have an idea," Carol said. "Leave your coats on and go out to the gazebo."

"What for?" Jenny asked, puzzled.

"Just do it, okay? All of you - go!"

The three of them went out the back door, taking the dog with them. The lights twinkled around the gazebo and the snow was still falling; a little heavier, now. Doug was sure he would have to shovel the walks in the morning.

"What are we suppose to do out here, Dad?" Jenny wondered, as they brushed snow off the seats in the little structure and sat down.

"I'm not sure, Jen. Let's wait and see. Maybe she has a surprise for us," he said.

Soon the back porch light went on and they could see her coming down the stairs, carrying a tray. Sadie ran to meet her.

"Be careful, girl. I don't want to drop this," she said, avoiding the dog who was running just ahead of her.

Doug stood up to give her a hand with the tray she was carrying. "What is this?" he asked.

"Hot cocoa and Christmas cookies," she told him. "I thought it would be nice to have it out here."

"Cool, Mom. It's a good idea!" Jenny said, reaching for a warm mug.

"Try not to get anything on your coat, Troy," Carol told her son.

"This is really nice, Mom," Doug said. "And these cookies are great!" he added, knowing that the kids had helped her make them. "We'll leave some out for Santa, right?"

"Right!" Troy said, with his mouth full.

"Yes, we should," Jenny said, with some doubt. She was having trouble believing that a fat old man, dressed in red, rode through the night sky on a sleigh pulled by animals that were not meant to fly, but she didn't want to express her doubt just yet. When she was younger, she hadn't thought about how illogical it really was. She was growing up.

They finished the cocoa and most of the cookies

and sat watching the falling snow.

"Well, I think we'd better go in and get ready for bed," Carol told them. "It's getting late." They had their baths before going to church, so they could just brush their teeth and go to bed. It was nearly eleven o'clock. The kids were rarely up this late, but tonight was special, and they would sleep later the next morning - their parents hoped.

When the kids were settled in bed, Carol welcomed the time alone with Doug. They were sitting on the couch, sipping wine and enjoying the peace of the season. Soft music played on the stereo. The gifts from Santa had been placed under the tree, and cookies and milk were left by the fireplace. Everything was ready for morning

"I'm so much happier now that Sarah's gone," she told him, meaning no disrespect, but it had been a difficult time for her. Now she could relax, care for her family, and enjoy this beautiful old house.

He reached behind him and brought out a small box, wrapped in gold paper and ribbon. "This is for you," he said, handing it to her.

"Well, I wonder what this could be," she said, shaking it. "Hmmm, I wonder." She took off the ribbon, removed the paper and opened the box. "Oh, I love them!" she exclaimed, when she saw the pearl earrings. "They're perfect," she said, as she turned on the lamp, so she could get a better look. "Thank you, Dear," she said, giving him a kiss.

She put the earrings in her ears and got down on her hands and knees to reach under the tree. "This one's for you," she said, handing him a large box

Sarah

that was wrapped in red and green paper.

He took it and put it on his lap. "They look nice on you," he said, pointing to the earrings.

She tucked her hair behind her ears so they would show, and went to the mirror in the front hall to see for herself. "I really like them," she said, coming back to where he sat. "Open it!" she told him, sitting down on the couch next to him.

He pulled the wrapping off the box and removed the cover. "Oh, this is nice," he said, holding up the thick woolly sweater. He pulled it over his head. It fit perfectly. "There's more," she told him. A black leather wallet lay in the sweater box.

"Oh, I need this," he said, laughing. His wallet was very worn and beginning to fray, but he liked the way it fit the curve of his hip when he carried it in his back pocket.

"I wish I had more for you," she said.

"More? What for?" he asked. "You, my dear, are the best gift of all," he told her, seriously.

"The sweater looks good on you," she said. "I hope you like it."

"I love it! Thank you," he said, kissing her and taking off the sweater. It was a bit warm with it on, in front of the fire. "Would you like more wine?" he asked.

"No, I don't think so. Do you know what time it is?"

He didn't, and looked at his watch. "I had no idea it was this late. We'd better go up," he said, then reached under the cushion. "Look what I found!" he said, with feigned surprise.

"What is it?" she asked.

"How should I know. Why don't you open it," he suggested. It was a small gold box exactly like the one that the earrings had come in.

She smiled at him and started taking off the wrapping. "What have you done? The earrings are plenty," she told him, as she took the lid off the little box. "Oh, Doug, it's lovely!" she exclaimed, as she held it up. It was a delicate gold chain bracelet, with nine pearls the same size as the earrings, that were evenly spaced along its length. She quickly undid the clasp and put it on her wrist; it was a bit tricky as it was a safety clasp, but she did it. "It's absolutely beautiful. I love it," she told him and kissed him again. "I'm sleeping with my jewelry on tonight!" she announced, as they picked up the wrapping paper and wine glasses.

"I almost forgot. We'd better do something with the milk and cookies," he said.

"Oh, I'm glad you said that," she said, having completely forgotten about it. She took the glass and plate into the kitchen, where she poured the milk down the sink and put the cookies back in the tin - remembering to crumble part of one on the plate before returning it to the living room. She crumpled up the napkin and set it on the table by the fireplace.

"Looks legit," he said, blowing out the candles.

"I guess that's it, then," she said, looking around to make sure all the candles were out. "I wonder if Sadie needs to go out one more time," she muttered.

"She was outside with us, remember? She'll be okay 'til morning," he said. "Let's go to bed. I'm beat."

Sarah

"Me, too," she said, yawning. "Big day tomorrow."

He followed her up the stairs where they quietly got ready for bed. They checked on the kids; both were sleeping. Sadie was at the foot of Troy's bed, and she was dreaming. Her legs were twitching; she was chasing something, probably a rabbit, or the cat. Sophie was ensconced exactly in the center of their bed, with one paw covering her eyes. Carol carefully picked her up and moved her to the end of the bed, where she settled herself again and began to purr, softly.

"Thank you, again, for my pearls," she whispered, when they were in bed. "I really love them."

"You're welcome, again, and thank you, too. I love you," he said, quietly.

"Me, too, and Merry Christmas," she said, hoping the kids wouldn't be up at the crack of dawn.

~17~

They didn't wake until eight o'clock on Christmas morning. They all would have slept longer, but Sadie needed to go out and Sophie was looking for her breakfast.

"Well, good morning, and Merry Christmas to you both," Carol said, quietly to the animals as she put on her robe and slippers.

"What time is it?" Doug asked, groggily.

"It's eight o'clock," she told him. "I can't believe they aren't up yet. I'll go make the coffee."

"I'm up," he said, swinging his legs out of bed and planting his feet on the floor. He ran his hands through his hair and sat for a minute before getting up and walking across the hall to the bathroom. He heard the kids giggling in the hall as he brushed his teeth. "Wait for me," he called to them, around his toothbrush.

Carol was in the kitchen, when they all came bounding down the stairs. "Merry Christmas!" she called to them.

"Merry Christmas, Mom!" they answered from the other room.

"Mom, come here and see what he brought us!" Troy shouted.

"I'm coming," she said, going into the living room with two mugs of coffee. She gave one to Doug and sat on the edge of the couch.

"Oh, look. Just what I wanted!" Jenny said, opening the latest Barbie doll. "Isn't she pretty, Mom?"

"She certainly is," Carol said.

"Look, Mom," Troy said, excitedly. "I can build a whole world with these!" He had been asking for the set of building blocks for a long time.

They had opened all the toys from Santa, when Jenny noticed Carol's bracelet.

"Where did you get that, Mom?" she asked.

"From Daddy," she said, showing it to her daughter.

"You got Mom a bracelet?" Troy asked his dad, with a worried look on his face.

Doug glanced at Carol and she read his look. Her son had gotten her the same gift.

"You know I haven't had a bracelet since I was a little girl. I really like them again. I wish I had more," she said, casually.

Troy covered his mouth with his hands and shrugged his shoulders. He knew he had gotten her just what she wanted. He raised his eyebrows and looked at his dad, knowing that he knew it, too.

"Now do you want to open your presents from us?" Jenny asked her parents.

"Absolutely, we do!" Doug told her. "And we have a couple here for you and your brother, too."

The kids got clothes and other small things that they had said they wanted. They were easy to buy for and happy with whatever they got. They thanked their parents with kisses and hugs and found the gifts they had bought for them under the tree.

"This is for you, Dad," Troy said, handing him a package. "And it's from me."

"Well, thank you," Doug said, and tore off the paper. "Just what I need! New hankies. And holy cow, they have my initials on them! How cool is that?"

"So you really like them, Dad?" his son asked.

"I really do, Troy. Thank you."

Carol loved the scarf from Jenny and knew it would be perfect with her coat. And Doug thought the necktie was a great choice.

"Now open this one, Mom," Troy said, sounding very proud. "I *know* you'll like this!"

She took off the wrapping and opened the box.

"Oh, I do like it very much!" she said, as she put the bracelet with the blue crystals on her other wrist.

"You said you wished you had more of them. So now you do," he told his mother, beaming. She hugged him and gave him a kiss.

"Thank you so much, Honey. It sure is pretty," she said.

"We almost forgot Sadie and Sophie!" Jenny exclaimed, looking around the room for them. She went to find the cat and Doug whistled for the dog. Sadie came running, but the cat wasn't very interested. Jenny ran upstairs and returned carrying Sophie, who looked pretty perturbed at having her mid-morning nap interrupted.

The kids opened the presents for their pets, and Sadie happily chewed the rawhide bone, but Sophie turned away from the little catnip mouse and silently went back upstairs to finish her nap.

"She'll find her present later and play with it, Jen," Carol told her.

Everyone was happy with what they had been given and chattered excitedly as they looked at each gift again.

Carol started picking up wrapping paper and thinking about breakfast. "We should eat something, soon," she said.

"Let's have brunch," Doug suggested. "Aren't you planning dinner around two o'clock?"

"I told Don to come over about two; we'll probably eat by two-thirty. Brunch sounds like a good idea," she said.

"Do I like it?" Troy asked. "I never had any brunch before."

"Brunch is when you eat breakfast and lunch together," Doug told him.

Troy thought for a minute. He sure had never heard of that.

"So if you eat lunch and supper together, is it called lupper?" he wondered. It made perfect sense to him.

They cleaned up the living room and Doug started a fire in the fireplace. They would keep it burning until late tonight, on this very special day.

Doug started in the kitchen and Carol was upstairs making up the beds when Jenny came running up the steps.

"Mom, come quick. You have to see Dad!" she said, laughing.

"Oh, now what's he doing?" Carol asked, and followed her daughter downstairs. She could hear the chorus of Jingle Bells being sung off-key in the kitchen. Troy was standing in the kitchen doorway, pointing to the pantry and trying to stifle his laughter with his other hand.

There stood their dad, in his shorts and T-shirt, with the tie Jenny had given him, backwards on his head, whisking eggs in a bowl, and singing Jingle Bells for all he was worth.

"What on earth are you doing?" Carol asked, laughing as she walked into the kitchen. The kids were right behind her giggling and asking the same question.

"What *are* you doing, Dad?" Jenny said, full of laugh.

"I am preparing brrrrrunch, Madam!" he told her, pulling the tie around to the side of his head and making a face.

Troy couldn't stop laughing at that, and his mother just threw up her hands.

"When did this place turn into a loony-bin?" she asked, turning to go back up to finish the beds. She couldn't stop laughing either. She hadn't felt this light-hearted in a long time.

"Brunch will be served in ten minutes, everyone!" he called to them in a very strange voice.

~~~

They ate in the kitchen as the dining room was set for Christmas dinner. Doug had put on his robe and taken the tie off his head.

"This is very tasty," Carol said, smiling at him.

"Thank you, Dear," he said. "After this, I have to shovel the sidewalks. Anybody want to help?"

"I have to get dinner," Carol said.

"I'll help you, Dad," Troy told him. Jenny wanted to stay inside.

"Before we go out, Troy, I think we should call Grandma and Grandpa," Doug said, as he threw another log on the fire.

They all gathered around the phone so each one could have a chance to talk to Doug's parents. Troy talked first, telling them what Santa had brought him and that Don was coming for dinner. Bye, Grandma! Bye, Grandpa," he yelled into the phone and handed it to his sister.

"Hi, Grandma. Oh, good . . . ." She stood quietly and listened for a few minutes, unlike her brother. "No, we didn't, Grandma. Not yet," Jenny said. Then covered the mouthpiece with her hand. "They mailed our presents a little late; we'll get them next week," she told her mother. "Oh, that's okay, Grandma. Merry Christmas! Love you, too," she said, and handed the phone to her dad. Doug took it and wished his parents a Merry Christmas. He talked a few minutes before giving the phone to his wife.

"Grandma says the nightgown fits perfectly, Mom, and Grandpa loves the shirt," Jenny told her mother as she waited for her turn on the phone.

Doug gave the phone to his wife and went into the living room with the kids.

"Grandma and Grandpa are hanging up now!" Carol called to them, after talking a few minutes. She held the receiver out and away from her ear.

"Bye, Grandma and Grandpa!" the kids called, loudly.

"Merry Christmas. We love you, too," Carol said and hung up the phone.

"They heard you say good-bye," she told the kids.

"Well, who didn't?" Doug said, putting on his heavy jacket. "Let's go, Buddy. Got your shovel?"

Sarah

~18~

The aroma of dinner began to fill the house. Jenny was helping her mother and playing with her new things in between chores.

"Well," Carol said, with her hands on her hips looking over the dining room.

"I think that's it. That's all we can do right now, Jen. Thank you for your help, Honey." The ham was in the oven, the potatoes were peeled, the vegetable dishes were ready for the oven and the fruit platter was in the fridge. "Let's see . . . rolls, butter, relishes, water glasses . . . ." she was thinking aloud. "Shall we go up and change our clothes, Jen?" Doug and Troy were still outside with the dog. The shoveling was done; now they were throwing snowballs for Sadie to catch in her mouth. She was pretty good at it, too.

Carol went out to the back porch and called to them. "You guys better come in soon and get changed. And be sure to take Sadie downstairs and get the snow off her feet."

"Okay, Mother!" they giggled, in unison.

When the dog played outside in the winter, snow

would get packed between the pads of her feet. At times she would stop and try to get it out with her teeth, but they found it easier if they helped her.

Carol went upstairs to get ready.

"Does this look okay, Mom?" Jenny asked. She had two new dresses to choose from.

"It sure does. That's just the one that I would have picked," Carol told her. "Do you need help with your hair?" she asked. Her daughter nodded, she did. She wore a blue dress, that brought out the color of her eyes, and today she wanted to wear her hair down with a headband that matched her dress. Carol brushed her daughter's hair and helped her put the headband in place.

"You look very pretty, Jen," she said.

"Thanks, Mom. So do you," she replied. All dressed and ready for Christmas, they went downstairs. They could hear the laughing and fooling around down the basement when they were in the kitchen.

"What's going on down there?" Carol called to them with much authority.

"Nothing, Mom," Troy said and they laughed more.

"You have to change your clothes. Don will be here soon!" she said.

"We seen him out shoveling. He's bringing a surprise," Troy yelled.

"It's not, I seen, or we seen . . ." she heard her husband say, and wondered what Don would bring.

At two o'clock, everyone was dressed and ready. Doug had even tied a red kerchief around Sadie's neck so she looked dressed up, too. She seemed to know that this was a special day and didn't object. Putting something on Sophie was a different story, however. Completely unadorned, she was regal, and she knew it.

When the doorbell rang, they all went into the hall to greet their guest.

"Merry Christmas, Don," Doug said, shaking hands with his neighbor.

"Merry Christmas, everyone!" Don said, as he set a shopping bag on the floor and started taking off his coat.

"Merry Christmas, Don. Let me take your coat for you," Carol said, and gave him a quick hug.

"What's in the bag, Don?" Troy asked.

"How about, Merry Christmas, Don, first, young man," his dad scolded.

"Oh, yeah. Sorry. Merry Christmas, Don," he said, shyly.

Don patted Troy on the head. "And the same to you, my friend," he said. "You look awful pretty, Jenny."

"Thank you, Don. It's new," Jenny said, holding the skirt of her dress out on each side so he could see it.

"And look at you, Sadie girl! You look pretty, too," he said, and scratched the dogs ears. "You're such a good girl," he told her, quietly. He had grown very fond of the dog and was happy to have her next-door. It was almost as nice as having a dog of his own.

"Don, please come in and make yourself at home," Carol told him, graciously, and led him into the living room.

"Well, first I should empty my bag, here," he said, picking it up from the floor.

"What have you got there?" she asked.

"Oh, not much, really. Just a little something for you and Doug and something for the kids. And a bottle of wine to go with dinner," he said, holding it up for her to see. "Or you can save it for another time, whatever suits you," he said, taking the wrapped packages out of the bag, and handing her the bottle of wine.

"Oh, I think we'll have this with dinner. It will taste good with the ham," she told him. "Thank you, Don, but you didn't have to bring anything, you know."

"I know, but I wanted to. Is that what smells so good? I haven't had ham in a long time," he said, looking around the living room. "Your house looks so nice, and that's a great looking tree."

"Thank you, we had fun decorating," Carol said, and excusing herself, went into the kitchen. Doug and the kids stayed with Don.

"Let us know if you need help out there," Doug called to her.

"I will," she answered.

Alone in the kitchen, she thought about how wonderful her life was in this house and tried to imagine what Sarah's life had been like under the same roof. She shuddered, remembering the coroner's report, and took the vegetable dishes out of the oven. Dinner was ready.

~~~

The meal was delicious and everyone praised Carol, even the kids. When they were finished eating, they cleared the table and opted to have dessert later.

Don insisted on helping with the dishes, and he and Doug ended up in the pantry together. Don washed and Doug dried. Carol put away any leftovers and the kids went back to their new toys in the living room.

"This is so nice of you guys," Carol said, as she put the last of the leftover food in the fridge.

"It's the least we can do. You did all the cooking," Don said. "I'm so glad that you invited me, today."

"And we're so glad you could come," she told him.

"Yes, we are. It's great having you here," Doug said, as he put the dried plates in the cupboard.

"Well, it was a great dinner and I appreciate it," their neighbor said, looking around to see if there were more dishes to wash. "Are we done?"

"Yes," she said. "Thanks again. Now we can go and see what you brought us, Don. We have a little something for you, too."

"Oh, you didn't have to go and do anything like that. Just being here with you is enough," he said, sincerely.

"Kids! Should we give Don his present, now?" Carol asked.

"Yes," they said. "And can we open the ones he brought for us?"

The phone rang just as the kids were passing out the gifts. Jenny grabbed it, hoping it was Allison. "Mom, it's Uncle Tom!" she called to her mother, and then chatted excitedly with Carol's brother.

"Okay, Uncle Tom. Here's Mom. Good-bye," she said and gave her mother the phone.

"Tom! How nice to hear your voice . . . ." they talked for several minutes before she called Doug to the phone. "Thanks for calling. Think about next year, now. I know it's a long way off, but we have to plan or we won't do it. Okay. Bye now. Here's Doug," she said, and handed the phone to her husband.

"That was my brother. I'd love for you to meet him sometime, Don. We're all going to try to be together next Christmas, if we can. Doug's parents, too. I hope they can come and stay here with us for a few days," she told him.

They spent half an hour or so opening their gifts. The gloves fit Don perfectly. It had been a good guess, Troy said.

Don gave Jenny a doll with different changes of clothes. Not a baby doll, but a girl doll; she looked about the age of Jenny.

"Thank you, Don! I love her! Look at the clothes, Mom. Isn't she pretty? Oh, thank you, Don," she said, again and went over to him and hugged him.

"You're so welcome, Jenny," he said, looking pleased that she had given him a hug.

Troy was pulling off the wrapping of his package and was delighted, too, when he saw that it was a remote controlled race car.

"Dad, look at this!" he said, excitedly. "Thank you very much, Don. How does it work?"

Don reached in his pocket and took out the batteries that were needed. "I didn't think of these until after I'd wrapped it," he told them, handing

Sarah

the batteries to Troy. "Give them to your dad, he'll show you how it works."

The batteries were put in and the instructions read. Troy went out to the kitchen to play with it on the hard floor, and Jenny went upstairs to call her friend, Allison.

"If they have company, Jen, don't talk long," Carol told her.

Don had taken a picture of the kids with Sadie and Sophie out in the backyard, a couple months before. It was beautiful, with all the fall colors. He'd had it enlarged, matted and framed to give to his neighbors for Christmas.

"This is so good, Don," Doug said, holding it up. "How did you get them all to sit still?" he asked, laughing.

"What a nice gift, Don. Thank you so much!" Carol said, admiring the photograph.

"I just took it on a whim," he told them. "They were out in the backyard and I thought I'd like to have a picture of all of them, but when I saw how nicely it turned out, I thought you'd like one, too."

"It's very good, and so thoughtful, Don. Thank you, again," Carol said, and put it on the table by the couch. "The kids will like it, too," she said. "Who's ready for dessert? Shall I put on some coffee?"

~~~

She had made a gingerbread cake as she did every year for Christmas. She served it with mounds of whipping cream on top.

"This is a birthday cake, actchaly," Troy said, licking the sweet cream from his fingers. "Today is a special birthday," he told Don.

"That it is," Don said, smiling at Carol and trying to remember if he knew anyone else who had a birthday cake on this special day. "It's a very nice gesture."

The kids finished dessert and went back to their play. The adults sipped coffee and talked together in the living room.

"I'm sure glad we got that Sarah business taken care of," Don said, soberly.

"So am I! I feel so much better, now . . . I just can't tell you," Carol said.

"Yeah, it was rough there for a while," Doug agreed. "And I want to thank you again for the help, Don. I don't think I could have done it myself."

They talked about their incredible experience, still finding it hard to believe.

"I think it will remain a mystery, forever," Carol said, softly.

Sarah

~19~

"Mom, could Allison stay overnight again before we go back to school?" Jenny asked, as they ate breakfast the morning after Christmas. They had slept late and were having a quiet morning. Doug was back to work.

"Sure, Jen. You have more than a week left of your vacation. Isn't that great? We'll have to think of something fun to do," Carol told her.

"I wanna make a snowman," Troy said, chasing the last few Cheerios that were floating in the milk left in his cereal bowl. "Is there enough snow, Mom?" he wondered.

Carol was finishing her coffee and trying to read the morning paper. "Enough what, Honey?" she asked.

"Snow, Mom. He wonders if there is enough snow to make a snowman," Jenny said.

"Well," Carol said, folding up the newspaper and looking out the window. "There's a lot of it out there. If it's good packing, I'm sure we could. I thought maybe we could go for lunch one day, and go shopping or to a movie," she teased, knowing what her son thought about shopping with his mom and sister.

"Movie! A movie, not shopping!" he exclaimed.

"Maybe Allison could go, too, Mom. Or should we go alone?" Jenny asked.

"Let me think about it a bit," her mother said.

Carol felt lazy this morning. After all the holiday work, it felt good not to have the day planned. She poured a second cup of coffee and sat at the kitchen table watching Sophie, who was batting the catnip mouse around the kitchen floor.

"Well, you finally decide to give it a try, eh, Sophie?" she said, softly, to the cat. The kids had tried to interest her in the mouse, but she would have nothing to do with it. It was just her way. Sophie did things only if and when she wanted to. Carol smiled and watched her tuck the mouse close to her chest, somersault and then kick it away from her with her hind feet, only to chase it across the floor and repeat the whole action again. Sadie was lying on the rug by the backdoor. Her head rested on her paw, as she, too, watched the antics of the cat.

Jenny came into the kitchen, nearly running into Sophie as she shot across the floor in chase of the mouse. "Sophie! Watch out," she cried, "I almost stepped on you, silly."

"She likes her Christmas present, Jenny," Carol said, and rinsed her cup out in the sink. "I think today we'll just stay home and make plans for the rest of your vacation, okay?"

"Okay, Mom. I won't call Allison until we decide."

"Maybe you should call her, Jen. Find out what

Sarah

day is good for her, and we'll go from there," her mother told her.

~~~

The last week of their vacation went by quickly. Troy spent several days with his friend, Jason, at one or the other's house, and Jenny was busy with Allison. Jenny spent one whole day at her friend's house, and two days later Allison stayed overnight with Jenny. The two girls had lots of time to show each other what they got for Christmas, play with the toys and try on the clothes. They had such fun together.

One morning, Carol took the two boys and Jenny and Allison to the movies. After the movie was over, they picked up lunch and went home to eat, and then spent the rest of the day playing. The girls were upstairs and the boys occupied the downstairs and the basement. They were all very well-behaved kids and Carol didn't mind having them all in the house for the afternoon.

The boys played with the remote control car, that Don had given Troy, down in the basement much of the time.

"Okay if we move the rug from Sarah's spot, Mom?" he called from the bottom of the stairs. "The car gets stuck on it!"

"Yes, that's fine," she answered. He always called the cement patch Sarah's spot. Carol wondered if he had any idea what had actually transpired down there. Oh, she was glad that was over . . . and Sarah was at rest.

When it was time to go home, the kids wished they could stay longer, but planned another day together instead.

~~~

New Years Eve was a quiet affair at 409 North Elm. The kids were told they could stay up until "Happy New Year" as Troy called it, but neither one of them was awake when the clock struck midnight. They had fallen asleep in their sleeping bags in front of the television.

"Should we leave them down here, or carry them up?" Doug asked.

"Let's put them in their beds," Carol said. "Then we'll be alone for a while."

"Good idea," Doug said, as he carefully picked up his daughter from the floor.

"Hi, Daddy," she said, half asleep, and closed her eyes again.

Carol went up ahead of them to open up the beds. "Sophie, could you move, please?" The cat was on Jenny's bed, and objected having to move, but did.

Sadie followed closely behind Doug as he carried Troy up to his bed. When they were both settled, their parents went back to the living room and threw another log on the fire. It was only eleven o'clock.

"Well, they lasted longer than I thought they would," Doug said, as he sat on the couch, watching the fire. In half an hour, they opened a bottle of sparkling wine and shared a plate of cheese and crackers. They watched the festivities on television as the world welcomed the new year.

"Happy New Year, Carol," he said, gently stroking her face and kissing her deeply.

"Happy New Year," she whispered, softly, returning his kiss.

Sarah

~~~

Next morning, the Christmas decorations were taken down and put away. The bare tree was hauled out to the backyard and festooned with cranberries and popcorn that the kids had helped string.

"The birds will like this, don't you think, Troy?" Jenny asked.

"Yeah, I think so."

"Mom says we can watch them from the window," she told him.

The new year had begun, and tomorrow the kids would be back in school. They all seemed eager to begin this year of surprises, especially Carol. She was happy to be in this wonderful old house and grateful that she no longer had Sarah in the basement. What an experience that had been. At times she thought maybe she had dreamed it, being a skeptic and all, but knew she hadn't.

And so it was, the family at 409 North Elm was involved with the business of living, and the little girl named Sarah no longer stood in the shaft of light in the cellar. She rested peacefully in her humble grave beneath the marker made of bronze.

The End

About the Author

K. M. Swan started writing when she was in her fifties. After High School she trained as a registered nurse, married, raised four children and practiced nursing part-time. She now has three grandchildren and enjoys writing about things that are important to her.

The Novels of K. M. Swan

If you enjoyed reading *Sarah* and would like additional copies or information about other novels:

- *The Loft*
- *Catherine's Choice*
- *The Journals*

Please mail your request to:

K. M. Swan
P.O. Box 8673
Rockford IL 61125

E-mail: KMSwanbooks@aol.com

Or check your local bookstore for availability.